THE AUSTRALIAN CLASSICS LIBRARY

Tales of the Early Days

Price Warung

Introduction by Laurie Hergenhan

General editors
Bruce Bennett, University of New South Wales
Robert Dixon, University of Sydney

SYDNEY UNIVERSITY PRESS

Published 2009 by Sydney University Press

SYDNEY UNIVERSITY PRESS
Fisher Library, The University of Sydney
www.sydney.edu.au/sup

First published in 1894 by George Robertson and Co., London

This, the Australian Classics Library text of *Tales of the Early Days* is a repaging of text files on SETIS, themselves input from the 1894 edition published by George Robertson and Co., London

© Introduction by Laurie Hergenhan 2009
© Sydney University Press 2009

The publication of this book is part of the University of Sydney Library's Australian Studies electronic texts initiative. Further details are available at http://purl.library.usyd.edu.au/sup/oztexts

Front cover image: portrait of William (Price Warung) Astley, courtesy of the Mitchell Library, State Library of NSW

ISBN 978-1-920899-05-9

For current information see http://purl.library.usyd.edu.au/sup/9781920899059

Contents

Introduction

Price Warung's historical tales, written just over a hundred years ago, have dropped from readers' attention. It is time to reconsider what they have to say to a twenty-first century audience. White Australian history has been attractive to writers and readers from the early days of white settlement. Indeed, the degree of interest in the history is in inverse proportion to its relatively short length. Marcus Clarke's title, *Old Tales of a Young Country* (1871), suggests that a young country can have an interesting past. The same ambiguity is contained in the dual conception of Australia, as both a new country and an old one. Of course recent re-assessments of Aboriginal history and pre-history have enlarged perspectives enormously. Before this change two main elements in the past attracted fiction writers: on the one hand pioneering of the land, along with building a new society and, on the other, convictism as a dark stain on our history. The positive achievement of the first, and the shame of the second, represent two enduring themes.

Historical fiction in popular literature and film allows for the exploitation of the 'foreignness' of the past by a concentration on strange and extreme happenings far distant from the mundane realities of the present. Serious writers look beyond romance to seek essential truths. They use literal fact but are not bound to it in the way historians are. As Thomas Keneally, author of the convict novel *Bring Larks and Heroes* (1967), commented, 'the novelist need not prove his reliability to scholars ... the only warrant a writer needs for his ideas about the past is that they reek of human, poetic, dramatic, symbolic veracity and resound in his imagination.' Similarly, Warung at his best is primarily concerned with imaginative truth, 'symbolic veracity,' though he draws on documentary fact and social realism.

The present out of which authors write shapes their pictures of the past. Warung wrote his ninety-four stories for the Sydney *Bulletin* in the early 1890s. Under its editor, J.F. Archibald, this influential magazine was strongly nationalist, egalitarian and anti-British in the lead-up to Federation. Warung shared these views, expressing them more overtly in his crusading journalism. Very little is known of him and his family. They migrated to Australia when he was four and he may have resented the dislocation or 'coming down in the world.' From the age of twenty-three he had a history of nervous breakdowns. He also suffered from a form of tertiary syphilis, becoming addicted to morphine. There is evidence enough here, apart from his politics, or perhaps in combination with them, to account for his attraction, almost addiction to the dark suffering of the convict system, which bred bitterness and revenge in its victims and perhaps stimulated answering feelings in its chronicler.

Whatever personal traits helped to shape Warung's tales, they must be judged on their own merits as fictions. They share with other fiction of social protest a common strategy: a concentration on the worst, on extremes, using these as more deeply revealing of the spirit behind a social abuse and as heightening a story's impact. This imaginative licence resembles putting human beings under a magnifying glass so that certain aspects will stand out. Historians have long exposed as myth the view of convicts as 'more sinned against than sinning.' But myths are not easy to kill off. As I write this introduction in 2008 two kinds of history continue to appear, either debunking the myth by stressing the positive effects of the system or contributing to it by concentrating on spectacular abuses. The shame that lurks behind the triumphalism of many nationalist histories was for long concentrated on the so-called convict stain. It displaced guilt over the reality of the more widespread and continuing injustices to Aborigines which has only surfaced recently. Even a crusading magazine like the *Bulletin* was racist, using as its banner headline, 'Australia for the white man.' Promoters of an 'Australian legend' of egalitarianism and solidarity have enlisted Warung's tales as evidence that the convict system bred these qualities, but his stories show rather that brutalisation bred betrayal and self-interest.

'The Secret Society of the Ring' is one of Warung's best stories, drawing upon a blend of documentary realism, mystery, dramatic confrontation, horror and social fable. It is carefully constructed in four interlocking parts, rising to a crescendo of 'doom.' The story deals with the convict system (referred to as 'the System') for worst offenders on Norfolk Island and with the convicts' own retaliatory counter-system of the Ring, built up in revenge. The latter is constructed as a savage and obscene parody of the former. The Ring even distorts religious ritual showing that religion, supposedly the cornerstone of society, is coopted by both sides. Details of fact and figures are frequently cited. This builds up confidence in the narrator as having privileged access to the inner workings of both systems—he is an insider moving freely between two worlds, showing that they are hopelessly opposed. The detailed workings of the Ring persuade us to believe in, or to suspend our disbelief in the macabre events. It also shows that both sides are pawns, trapped in the machinery of convoluted rules and regulations.

In 'The Ring' Warung probes more deeply into the System and the minds of gaoled and gaolers alike than in his other stories. For this purpose he opposes convict views, particularly those of Ring members, to those of the chief administrator, Maconochie, who is based on the character of a famous penal reformer. Humane, well-intentioned officials are almost entirely missing from Warung's stories, but here he succeeds in bringing Maconochie alive without idealising him. Ironically in his attempt at reform he helps to bring about the deaths of two convicts he is trying to save. Moreover, in this sympathetic and subtle portrait Warung shows how idealists can be powerless to change the system because it is at heart corrupt and because even the well intentioned are unable to bridge theory and practice. Moreover Maconochie admits to self-interest: 'I wanted—well, I wished to count you as one of the trophies of my new methods' (72).

The clash between Ring member, Johnson, and Maconochie pierces to the heart of the System. It is basically corrupt because open to abuse: 'The System was not founded on justice. And in his heart Maconochie knew this was true ... British law proposed only to punish, not to give over the offenders to 'unusual punishment ... the taunt went home' (69). Maconochie feels powerless: 'Argument imperilled his authority. And, after all, *he* did not invent the system' (69). The story ends in a tragic stalemate: the Ring 'wins' in a black reversal of justice. The two victims, one meaning to sacrifice himself for the other, die for nothing. The System and Ring are perpetuated. The action of this aptly named story moves literally in a vicious circle.

'The Ring' belongs to a large body of protest literature, exposing horrors of the recent past, especially those concerning war, prison camps and closed institutions such as orphanages, mental hospitals and gaols, where officials abuse their power. Twentieth-century literature and film are full of such exposures, warnings meant to shock us into realisation of the excesses of human corruption. Warung's stories take an honourable place amongst such protest. If other stories in *Tales* present the world in unrelieved terms of black and white the complex 'The Ring' is his masterpiece. The story would lend itself to film with its effective crowd scenes interspersed with close-up confrontations, its mounting climaxes, its contrasting of light and dark, its undertow of doom. It moves the heart and grips our imaginations.

Laurie Hergenhan
University of Queensland

References

Andrews, B. *Price Warung*. Boston: Twayne Publishers, 1976.

Andrews, B.G. ed. *Selected Stories of Price Warung*. St Lucia: University of Queensland Press, 1975. Reviewed by Elliott, B. *Australian Literary Studies*, 7, 1976, 336–37.

Hergenhan, L. *Unnatural Lives: Studies in Australian Fiction about the Convicts*. St Lucia: University of Queensland Press, 1983, reprinted in 1993.

Hirst, J.B. *Convict Society and its Enemies*. Sydney: Allen & Unwin, 1983.

McQueen, H. *A New Britannia*. Victoria: Penguin, 1970.

Maxwell-Stewart, H. *Closing Hell's Gates*. Sydney: Allen & Unwin, 2008.

Palmer, N. 'Fourteen years.' Melbourne: Meanjin Press, 1948. Reprinted in Smith, V. ed. *Nettie Palmer*. St Lucia: University of Queensland Press, 1988.

Palmer, V. *The Legend of the Nineties*. Melbourne: Melbourne University Press, 1966.

Smith, B. *Australia's Birthstain*. Sydney: Allen & Unwin, 2008.

Ward, R. *The Australian Legend*. 2nd ed., Melbourne: Melbourne University Press, 1966.

TALES OF THE EARLY DAYS

BY

PRICE WARUNG

GEORGE ROBERTSON AND COMPANY

LONDON   MELBOURNE   SYDNEY

ADELAIDE   BRISBANE

1894

[Facsimile of first edition titlepage]

Note

For the purposes of these stories the epoch of the 'Early Days' is presumed to end with the cessation of transportation to Western Australia.

CAPTAIN MACONOCHIE'S 'BOUNTY FOR CRIME'

I.

THE most remarkable experiment, all things considered, ever made with the noble purpose of reforming criminals was Captain Maconochie's attempt to adapt his 'mark' system to the monstrous conditions of penal life at Norfolk Island. And being in principle humane, and in method an arraignment of all notions current in British and Colonial officialdom, it met with precisely that degree of success which was prophesied for it by Mr.—not then 'Sir'—E. Deas-Thomson, Colonial Secretary of New South Wales.

'Speaking, your Excellency,' said that venerable if somewhat pragmatical gentleman to Governor Sir George Gipps, 'from a lengthened experience of—h'm!—convict disciplinary methods, I have—ah!—no hope that Captain Maconochie's system will achieve the least good. It *must* fail, sir!'

And fail it did. To the undisguised delight of the Colonial Secretary's Office, Sydney, and the Deputy Commissariat-General's Departments of Sydney and Norfolk Island, it failed. You see, the first maxim of the Captain was the reformation of the criminal, while almost every other person connected with the System, from Lord John Russell to the meanest scourger on the Island or at Port Arthur, thought the criminal was a mere thing to be locked up, and fettered, and flogged into purity of life and integrity of conduct.

Now, Maconochie's success would have meant the System's condemnation. And his failure meant that the System was right and its administrators were wise. Therefore the failure was only to be expected. Men do not care about being proved wrong, even if it could be shown that a few dozen souls were saved in the process of correction.

For instance, Mr. Assistant-Deputy-Commissary-General Shanks would have had to confess himself egregiously in error had Convict Tobias Tracey, per ship *John*, third trip, kept continuously on the path of rectitude which Captain Maconochie marked out for him. And that was not to be thought of. Convict Tracey had to fall once more in the slough of ill-doing in order to prove A.D.C.G. Shanks right.

To enable you to understand how terrible was that fall we must measure the height which he had attained. Step by step, climbing upwards, now taking firm foothold on a dead sin, now clutching such aid as came from the opportunity to do a kindly service to a brother-felon; again slipping back into the pit of corruption because a messmate jeered at him; yet again striving against the tremendous alliance of the forces of evil, till he gained a new standing-place on the up-track—this was the history of Tracey during 1840, and the early part of 1841. In the later part of '41 he fell—thanks to A.D.C.G. Shanks—irretrievably. In the early months of '41, he had first come under the notice of the Captain-Superintendent, and had begun to aspire towards a manlier existence. During the interval between those first tentative strugglings to mount, and that last dreadful fall, his life was epic in its storms and its battles, its victories and its defeats.

II.

Look at his record.

His original conviction was on the 8th September, 1831, at a London gaol delivery. His crime was burglary, and his sentence, transportation for life.

His sojourn in the hulk obtained for him the distinction of 'a bad report,' and the voyage out to Sydney gave him still higher rank in the aristocracy of vice. 'He was doomed,' the Surgeon-Superintendent of the *John* (third trip) told him one day in mid-ocean, 'to become a Black Norfolker as sure as Fate.'

And Fate is unerring, as every one knows. Two years after landing in Sydney, he was sentenced by the Supreme Court for highway robbery and housebreaking. Once more his time was life, with the added distinction of irons—irons always—sleeping, waking, at work and at his meals—irons to be knocked off only if he mounted the scaffold, or on freedom coming to him otherway—say, through some kindly shot or kindlier blow. Freedom by process of servitude would never come to him. He was destined by Nature as a Retrograde.

Chaplain Taylor spoke of his 'Retrogrades' to Governor Gipps.

'Your "Retrogrades"? What are they?'

'Men who are further away from freedom each succeeding day they are on the Island—who are never nearer freedom than when they set foot here!'

'But, Mr. Taylor, in the nature of the case such characters must be few?' rejoined his Excellency.

'Few, your Excellency? Sixty out of each hundred!'

Now, at the precise moment the Superintendent's clerk at the Island gave a receipt to the master of the *Governor Phillip*, from Sydney, for the body of Tobias Tracey, No. 33–149, per *John* (3), that hardened villain might have expected release in twenty-five years, if the devil and the System would only allow him to keep his hands from picking and stealing, and breaking-in stores and warders' heads. Being predestined, however, to the ranks of the Retrogrades, within twenty-four hours of his arrival he was no nearer than thirty years to his freedom. He had knocked a gaol-turnkey down.

*　　　*　　　*

In 1835 his 'police history' was extended by five offences of the serious order. 'Light offences' were invariably at this period, and till the arrival of Maconochie, sentenced 'on view.' 'On view' punishments—that is, without trial—are supposed to have numbered, during 1833-4-5-6-7-8, between 8000 and 9000. They were never recorded; formal trials only were recorded; and these last during the years specified totalled 2483, and the awful mutiny year calendar was embraced in this sum. Of these trials Tracey was responsible, in 1835, for five.

In 1836 he was credited with four. The circumstance that he was ironed in gaol for the major part of this year accounted for the diminution of 20 per cent in the number of his heavy offences. When a felon was double-ironed in a 6 x 4 cell, when his right hand was manacled to a staple in the wall, when he saw a human face four times daily for ten seconds each time, it cannot be said that his opportunities for outraging the peace of the realm were numerous. Still, he enlarged his record by four entries.

In 1837 they varied his gaol privileges by flogging him, and the scourging-ground was the best place possible for adorning a man's record. He had only to swear at the superintending officer to be credited with another crime; and if, also, he struck the honourable scourger with his fist or head, or bestowed upon that official a sadly-needed kick, well, there was a second offence on the same day. Consequently, Mr. Tracey, who was in gaol from January to 7th March, was in gaol again from 3rd April 'till further orders.' In June and July he was in gaol, but in September he must have been out of gaol, for he absconded. He was arrested three-quarters of an hour afterwards at the gate of the Superintendent's quarters—said he had never been out of the gaol precincts—nevertheless, was presented with 300 lashes in one dose. And from 14th October onwards to the end of the year he was in gaol again, his record for the year being seven crimes.

In 1838 a variation in policy took place once more. He added no more than five offences to his history, but one of these earned him 100 lashes, and another four months in the sweet seclusion of his iron-cells—and the others? Each won for him a long term of 'solitary.'

The second Earl of Limerick, then plain Mr. Pery, and a humble 'Superintendent of Agriculture' on the Island, spent a brief space in one of the same solitary cells. He stayed till it was a question of his going mad, or going out. He went out, and found that he had been secluded 17 minutes! Tracey had three terms—14, 14, and 20. Minutes? No—days!

III.

As for Tracey's 1839 record, here it is as full as the books give it. There are no 'sentences on view' included, and he must have had his full share of them. You will not fail to notice the dreadfully heinous character of the recorded crimes.

DATE.	OFFENCE.	PUNISHMENT.
1839.		
Jan. 8.	Loitering on the road to and from his work.	To sleep in gaol one night.
Feb. 13.	Going to the hospital twice this day under false pretences, and incorrigible.	To gaol until further orders.
March 18.	Absent without leave and present at a fight.	To sleep in gaol one night.
March 22.	Assaulting and striking a fellow-prisoner.	Handcuffs all day.
March 23.	Refusing to join his gang when ordered by overseer.	Two days in gaol.
March 25.	Going to hospital without sufficient cause.	One month in gaol.
April 10.	Attending hospital on false pretences.	25 lashes.
April 13.	Attending hospital and subsequently refusing to work.	Gaol, on bread and water, till he goes to work.
May 4.	Refusing to work.	14 days' gaol, bread and water.

DATE.	OFFENCE.	PUNISHMENT.
1839. May 21.	Neglect of work.	Reprimanded conditionally.
May 27.	Absconding with three others, breaking open and entering the dwelling of Coxswain Segsworth, putting the inmates in fear, and resisting and wounding several constables and others to apprehend him.	300 lashes.
June 10.	Refusing to work.	50 lashes and bread and water till he goes to work.
June 14.	Refusing to work.	Gaol, on bread and water, as before stated.
June 26.	Refusing to work.	To receive only half ration of animal food.
Aug. 8.	Refusing to work.	50 lashes and bread and water till he goes to work.
Sept. 4.	Going to hospital on false pretences.	25 lashes and bread and water till he goes to work.
Oct. 9.	Refusing to work.	Reprimanded conditionally.
Nov. 9.	Making noise in gaol.	Three days' solitary confinement on bread and water.
Nov. 29.	Refusing to go to work, stating he was not able.	Bread and water till he is able.

At the end of 1839, with a double-life conviction over him, Tobias was exactly 53 years distant from freedom. But in February of the succeeding year Captain Maconochie arrived, and, to the amazement of the well-informed officers of the System as before established, almost immediately chose that prime rascal by the *John* (3) for special experiment. As soon as the new Super. was possessed of Tobias Tracey's police record, he ordered the man's irons to be struck off. Now, Major Bunbury, the previous commandant, had never dared approach Tobias except under the escort of two soldiers.

But the amazement of the staff was nothing to the surprise of the notorious fellow himself.

'Lord! what a fool the new 'un is if he thinks as he's got a softy to deal wi.'' Thus he laughed with a coarse mockery, as he passed into the Super.'s presence.

The Superintendent's tall and erect form filled the doorway of the Grass Hut where he was holding a preliminary inspection. In a few weeks he would turn the hut into a school and a Catholic chapel, but at present he proposed to use it as a court-house. 'Why?' The old officials asked the question—and cackled hilariously when they received the answer. So that prisoners for trial, who might have been in the local court before, might not be unpleasantly reminded of their past misdeeds! 'I want to start every man with a clean sheet as far as possible.' Laugh! Of course they laughed.

The Overseer in temporary charge of Convict Tracey saluted, and presented that ruffian. 'Transport Tracey, Tobias. No. 33-149, y'r Honour—bad k'racter—3 B's,[1] sir—suspected—'

'Of unnatural crimes—one murder—three burglaries—an' a heap t'other things, Super.—same ol' list,' concluded the convict himself. 'One o' th' worst men on th' Island, y'r Honour, now they've turned orf Westwood. There ain't a —— crime on the list, Super., that I ain't committed, 'cept

---

[1] 'Three B's.'—Trebly bad record.

those I'm goin' to commit. An' now yer know all, ol' cove! Give us my five hunderd quick an' 'a done wi' it. Look slippy now, Ol' King-o'-th'-lags!'

Accustomed as the penal officials comprising Captain Maconochie's little suite were to outbursts of reckless speech from the more hardened 'old hands,'[2] they scarcely expected Tracey to uncoil himself in this fashion, and they gazed curiously at Maconochie to note the effect of the speech upon him.

Two—three minutes elapsed before the Superintendent spoke. Tracey himself had expected an instant order for his removal to the triangles, and stood doggedly waiting for the command—which did not come.

All they saw was that Maconochie drew his handkerchief from his tail-pocket and blew his nose. Then—

'Let it be understood, Overseer—are you Overseer or Warder?'

'Overseer, sir—of the gaol-gang—Tuff, sir.'

'Very well, Overseer Tuff—let it be understood, if you please, that you are never to report a man's police-history till it is asked for by me directly.'

'Yes, sir!' answered the sub-official, with a sullen respectfulness. 'But 'twas the Majors reg'lashun, sir, wi' all transports, 'specially desp'rate ones!'

'Ho, ho! I be a desp'rate one, be I, Mr. Tuff?' grinned the transport. 'Well, I know I be—an' 'ere's to keep up th' k'racter.' With a mighty cuff he struck Tuff to the ground. 'There, Super. Macwot's-yer-name, give me my five hunderd lashes, an' 'a done wi' it, as I said afore!'

The ex-private secretary to noble Sir John Franklin answered the appeal. He stepped into the schoolroom, and called to the transport to follow him. Some of the officials who had looked on the incident just described would have entered likewise, but the Captain quietly waved them back.

---

[2] 'Old hand.'—At Norfolk Island this term had a different application to that given to it on the Continent in later days. It signified a 'doubly-convicted' convict—a prisoner with both a British and a Colonial sentence.

'I would prefer to be alone with this poor fellow, gentlemen. Excuse me for a few minutes,' he said.

'But, sir—the danger!' remonstrated A.D.C.G. Shanks.

The Captain smiled—not as, a few years later, John Price was wont to smile, with a lofty affectation of indifference to any possible danger that could threaten him—but pleasantly, as though he held an amulet bestowed by some good genius against evil.

Captain Maconochie might be a 'crank;' but, certainly, he was no coward.

IV.

As he walked in, Tracey had, obeying the mechanical instinct which, in spite of himself, the System had implanted in his nature, took his cap off. Then he recalled the act. He was not going to submit as 'a softy' to the new Super. Not he. He replaced the cap defiantly as he faced the Captain. However, the Superintendent gave no indication that he was aware of the insult. Bunbury would have chained Tracey down for the same deed.

'My man!' said Maconochie, 'I wish to have a talk with you!'

'I don't want to talk to yer! Come on an' flog me—or p'r'aps ye'd like to do th' nubbling cheat[3] trick at once? Better now than later. I'm boun' to come to it!' responded the callous wretch.

'Look, sir—' Maconochie paused. Till harassed by the incessant opposition of the old-time officials, Maconochie measured almost every word he uttered in a transport's presence. 'Constant dropping of water wears away a stone. The habitual use of forms of respect to any—even the most hardened—prisoner will insensibly, by wearing away the indurated surface, give his better nature room for play.' That was what he used to say.

'Look, sir—'

---

[3] 'The Nubbling Cheat Trick.'—Hang.

'*What!*' Lifer Tracey could not believe his ears. 'Sir! Wot a joke! Me with an "incorrigible" record—sir!'

'Look, sir—' Maconochie began again.

'None o' that foolin.' Yer not a-goin' to make a softy o' me, I tell yer!' Tracey raised his hand threateningly, as though in defence of that precious possession, his reputation for eminence in evil. 'I be'n't no parson's or Super.'s pet!'

'I am sure of it,' rejoined the Captain. 'But you are a man, and not a devil—I am sure of that as well!'

A second of wits-gathering silence. Then—

'No, I be'n't no man—a devil I am, or th' —— Systum hasn't done its work!' He laughed, with the reckless, sardonic laughter of the hopeless.

'No, you are a man, and no devil! And because you are a man, obey one of the first instincts of manhood, and that is to behave with respect to your just and legal superiors.'

'Just—legal!' Again the laugh—and then a storm of mad, tumultuous speech. 'Just is them wot justice do—legal is as legal act! Be'n't truth 'bove all things? Can a man be a man if he's a liar? Be'n't a liar allus a coward? An' no coward's a man? An' 'udn't I lie ef I paid respec' w'ere respec' be'n't doo? An' is respec' doo to unybody unner th' Systum, for wot cove is there unner th' Systum as acts justly, as acts legally? Answer me that, Ol' King-o'-th'-lags!'

'Poor man, poor man!' exclaimed Maconochie, and, pacing forward, he held out his hand. Tracey struck it aside passionately.

'Yer've left me nothin' but—oh, nothin,' nothin' but hate—an' now yer give me your pity. To the devil who made yer an' th' Systum!' He leapt tigerishly on the Superintendent—and was felled by a blow. There was nothing effeminate about Maconochie's muscles or his nerves, if there *was* just a suspicion of that quality attached to his judgment. No. 33-149 went down, and for a minute stayed down, dazed.

No word was spoken till Tracey, with eyeballs glaring redly instead of whitely, drew himself up to a sitting posture.

'Didn't I—say as the nubblin' cheat 'ud end it soon? By th' Lord, sir, I thank yer!'

Maconochie had faced a mutiny from a quarter-deck; had, as a lad, confronted, with only a toy-dirk in hand, a howling circle of barbaric mountain tribesmen thirsty for his blood; and yet, he was wont to say, never did human look appal him as that transport's glare of—gratitude.

'It's death—this—you know, my man?'

'Death 'tis an' welcome!' It was a hyena shriek made articulate.

'My *friend*, let me help you up!' Again Captain Maconochie stretched forth his hand.

Tracey looked up. 'D'yer mean it?' The softening of the words passed in the next instant from his face and tone. 'Mean it!' he continued, 'o' course yer mean it! Be'n't it yer dooty to 'and me to th' gallows!'

Maconochie pressed down his hand—lower—lower still—till it touched Tracey's shoulder.

'Tracey!' he whispered, 'Tracey! it is my duty to save you from—the gallows. That is why I am here. Tracey—let us be friends!'

No. 33-149—his agony wried his mouth as he spoke—simply repeated 'Friends!' and then bent his head upon his scarred hands. The upheaval of his universe had come, for, from the vortex of hell had sprung a voice—an *official* voice—that had uttered a kindly word. Kind words he had sometimes had before, but they were from clergymen; and the gospellers were bound to say something kind sometimes to earn their stipends.

While a man might draw twenty breaths he sat so, challenging his consciousness whether or no his world was altered. And then, from the core of the beast-nature with which the System had superseded that granted unto him by his Creator—John Price said once 'there were doubts as to the Creator, but there were none as to the System'—he spumed once more a torrent of volcanic hatred and suspicion.

'It's all a —— trap; yer think I be a double softy to be taken in so? Yer playin' the forgivin' to get time to call the guards, 'cos yer afraid I was a-goin' to kill yer! Oh, yer devil!'

He stood with parching lips and clenched hands, and the knots bulged on his temples as when a gymnast braces himself for a feat that will cause the heavens to resound either with Homeric plaudits or with his death-scream. Had he sprung, the help of soldier-guard would have come too late for the Super. But—

'Stay!' cried Maconochie. 'What proof do you demand that I am not the monster you fancy me? How can I show you my truth—that I mean to be as true a friend to every man here who will allow me as I can with God's help be—how can I do this?'

The appeal held Tracey in spite of himself. Scarcely knowing what he did, he gazed through the one window-space (unglazed) of the hut. Crossing the parade-ground leisurely were a lady and a maid-servant. A soldier followed them ten paces away. He pointed to them, and cried, hoarsely—

'Is that your wife?'

Maconochie's look followed the pointing-finger. 'Yes!' he replied.

'Then, I'll believe yer if—you—trust—her—your wife, I mean—in this room alone wi' me for five minutes by your watch.'

The Superintendent's face grew haggard in the tremendousness of the ordeal. But his soul answered to the test.

He went out—and said a few words to his wife. She went into the room, all unknowing, but believing utterly in her husband's wisdom.

V.

Maconochie lost, in the next moment, his composure. He thrust his watch into the hand of the soldier escorting the lady, and in the same action seized the man's musket.

'In four minutes—four minutes and a half—call "Time!"' he exclaimed, while he himself cocked the musket—and waited. So strained was his hearing to catch any sound from the room, that though but five yards distant from the group of officers, he did not hear Mr. Commissary Shanks say—

'Well—I'm damned! Maconochie's just offering a bounty for crime!'

*   *   *

He did not hear that, or indeed aught else, till the soldier cried, 'Time!' loudly. Then he started forward, but the appearance of his wife on the step momentarily arrested his rush. With the musket still in his hand, he ran to meet her. She motioned with her head. Through the doorway he saw—and heard—Tracey. The transport lay huddled, his head on the floor, his arms outstretched in the abandon of despair—or, remorse. And he was sobbing tearless sobs.

*   *   *

Not all at once did Tracey, after that supreme instance of trust, come back to the path of well-doing. His fight, however, against his past was strenuous.

It was in February that Captain Maconochie trusted him. And till the 23rd October of the year following, he kept almost a clear record. 'View' sentences had ceased entirely, and to the extreme disgust of the gentlemen possessing a more extensive acquaintance with the System than Captain Maconochie, Mr. Tobias Tracey declined to preserve by frequent attendances at court his average of 'offences needing formal trial.'

Mr. D.A.C.G. Shanks, on 23rd October, applied to the Superintendent for a trusty man to handle some stores.

And Mr. D.A.C.G. Shanks, being in an unbending, not to say affable mood, condescended to pass a pleasant word with the trusty man commissioned by the Super. to wait upon his Commissaryship.

'You're Tracey?'

'Yes, sir!' with a salute.

Mr. Shanks laughed. 'You're the man the Super. trusted the day after he took charge—trusted his wife with?'

There was a conscious pride in Tracey's voice as he replied, 'He did, sir!'

'Why, you donkey, he held a cocked musket in his hands all the time! Fine lot of trust in that, wasn't there?'

Convict Tracey was stunned. 'Are yer a-speakin' o' th' truth, sir?'

With a brutal oath, Mr. Deputy-Assistant-Commissary-General Shanks affirmed he was.

*   *   *

That same evening Tracey broke into Mrs. Whologhan's store with a crowbar.

SECRET SOCIETY OF THE RING

Part 1—The Convening of the Ring

I.

CAPTAIN Maconochie, who, with Major Anderson, supplied the non-demoniac element in the reigns of Norfolk Island Commandants, in pursuance of his theory that the convict should be encouraged to hope not alone for an alleviation of his physical condition, but also for 'a new moral nature,' hit upon an expedient for developing, even in hardened souls, those softening and refining tendencies which flow from a heart-felt solicitude for the welfare of others. By detaching transports into groups, or 'sub-gangs,' of three or five members, and holding each man of the three or five responsible for the good behaviour of his comrades, an irresistible appeal was at once made to the curiously-confused notions that swayed the average convict mind. An argument which had regard only to their own comfort or freedom from punishment would, in the case of nine out of ten 'old hands'—the doubly-convicted convicts transported from the mainland or Van Diemen's Land—be welcomed by an oath or a ribald jest. When callousness in infamy was deemed to be an honour—when irons were thought the insignia of chivalry—and 'connoisseurs in murder' felt it a privilege to take the hand of a 'locked-boot' victim—it was an insult to suggest an immunity from penalties as a reason for right action. Take another course, however, and appeal to the sense of fraternity, which seldom died out even in the 'best' men, and that caution in conduct and that eternal obedience to the regulations which a 'good' man would never think of exerting in his own interests, would be at once exercised for the benefit of his group-mates. Most of

Maconochie's attempts at penal reform sprang from his heart, and were seldom based on a hard, logical apprehension of facts as they were. But, in respect to his grouping system, his heart and his head acted together. His judgment and his experience of the 'old hands' taught him that it was literally and absolutely a point of honour with them never to procure punishment for another transport who manifested 'spunk.' And his heart showed him how to take advantage of this characteristic. What 'old hands' would not do for themselves they should do for others. They should respect regulations and official practices, because violation of them would cause the infliction of punishment upon their colleagues of the group.

Between the principal settlement (which was supposed to change its name according to the sex of the reigning sovereign, and, therefore, should have been called Queenstown in the present reign, but which, notwithstanding, was more often spoken of as Kings-town than Queenstown) and the outlying barracks at Longridge, the Commandant laid out, in March and April, 184—, a number of farms of six to ten acres each. On each farm a hut or cottage was erected, and a company of from three to five men was assigned to each hut and farm. For the first year, no rental was demanded by the Commandant. For succeeding years each group of tenants had to contribute a rental of twelve bushels of maize for each cleared acre, this quota being estimated to equal one-third of the average crop per acre raised by labour under direct taxation. And every group was constituted a 'mutual responsibility' sub-gang. That is to say, for the misdeeds of any one member of a group, the other members would suffer.

The group tenanting the hut on Section 5 B was constituted by some 'old hands' whose records were of the very 'best.'[1] Tested by the official standards of the elder System, they would have been welcomed by Lucifer with a 'Hail, fellows, well met!' And thereupon the soft-hearted

---

[1] At Norfolk Island it was the awful custom among the more hardened convicts to invert the meaning of 'good' and 'bad.' A 'good man' was a notorious criminal; a 'bad' one was a man who sought to act honestly and purely.

Commandant resolved they should have a chance to reform. Very much to the amusement of the Commissariat and other officials did he announce this determination.

The sub-gangers were five in number. Osborne, of whom we dare say no more than that it was a daily wonder to his comrades how he escaped hanging; Peake, a small-skulled, thirty-year-old lump of a physical deformity that rivalled his moral nature; a gentlemanly ex-forger who was popularly known as 'Barrington' from the circumstance that he knew off by heart the account of that immortal scoundrel's career; a 'Swinger'[2]—Felix—less sullen than brutish in feature, and of gigantic physical strength; and Reynell, a former soldier of the 'Fighting Half-Hundred,' who had been transported to Norfolk Island by a V.D.L. military court for desertion to Maori-land in a whaler.

A tall, strapping fellow, who carried himself with military erectness, was Reynell, and it was his boast that his parchment record was as long as himself. Of course, the assertion was a slight exaggeration, but Reynell was given to little whimsicalities. A devil when roused, he was, as a rule, a merry soul, who was pleasantly cynical. He entered into crime with the same zest as into a battle-square. 'It was but putting the bayonet into the law instead of the enemy,' he said to Mr. Pery, Superintendent of Agriculture, one day when Pery asked him why he would persist in setting the authorities at defiance. 'I have to let the devil out of me somehow, sir, and as her gracious Majesty—God bless her!—won't employ me against her enemies, I have to make enemies of my own. And the law's a grand enemy to fight, sir! It'll take such a lot of beating!'

Against a criminal of this temper the Law had used everything in its dread armoury, except 'the spread-eagle,' the gallows, and—a kind word and good faith. These last two instruments of unusual punishment Captain

---

[2] Transported for rick-burning—a follower of 'Swing,' the supposititious criminal who, at the period of the agricultural depression of the Early Thirties, was accused by the peasants of setting farmers' ricks and barns on fire.

Maconochie now determined to supply. He appointed Reynell leader of 5 B sub-gang at a Sunday morning 'after chapel' muster at the Iron Room.

'Henry Reynell, per *Coquette*, colonial transport,' called the mustering-overseer.

'Reynell, how do you come to be included among "old hands" when you're a "colonial"?' questioned the Commandant, with his pleasant resonance of voice, as soon as the man had replied with his 'Here!'

'The honourable Court gave me fourteen years, y'r Honour, and as I didn't think it enough I got 'em to make it life.' There was a ripple of laughter in the ranks.

'How?' asked the Captain, who took no notice of the demonstration.

'I struck the corporal of the Court guard—and so the honourable Court gave me what I wanted.'

'Not the same Court? It could not act at once and without being formally convened by the Colonel-Commanding?'

'As to that, sir, I can't say. All I know is that same Court convicted me—and I came here with a double sentence. Therefore, Major Ryan thought me entitled, sir, to all the emoluments, rights, and privileges of an old hand. I've been in irons all the time I've been here.'

'Will you take a word of advice from me, Reynell?' said the Commandant.

'Will—I—what, y'r Honour?' asked Reynell, with a choking breath in his voice that might have been amusement, or might have been sheer amazement at the autocrat of a penal settlement assuming so extraordinary a tone.

'Take my advice, my good fellow, just to drop that sneering manner of speech.' There was a genuine kindness in the words. Reynell drew himself up to his full height and clenched his fist. Those who stood by thought he was about to transform recklessness of tongue into madness of action. The line between a murderer and a hero is often but a hair's-breadth, and this man, who might easily become a hero, might as easily pass the line.

However, other answer than this he did not make. He flung out his closed hand and said—'So easy to preach, y'r Honour! With the iron in the soul, and the cat on the back, and the bayonet-point in the body, what wonder the sneer's on the lip? So easy for you gentlemen to deal with heartless *numbers.* You say, *Numbers* 37-189—that's me—and 39-204—that's Felix—don't *feel*. God above—don't we! And what weapon ha' we to fight the System with if you won't allow us to use our tongues? Even at our peril we must use 'em!'

He stopped and gathered strength for a last phrase which quivered with the under-thrill of his bitterness. 'It's fighting that's our last hope of keeping something of manhood to ourselves, sir! Fight!—I'd die if I did not fight—die or go mad!'

Outbursts of this sort were common enough among the more intelligent convicts, but Maconochie never ceased to be impressed by them. The receptive sympathy of the man—which proved his ruin as an administrator—was always stirred when the note of strength and sincerity ran through the transport's utterances. He listened now to Reynell with a patience that to his under-strappers and to the felons at muster seemed at once wonderful and childish.

With mutual nods and winks (in hearty enjoyment of the joke) the gentlemen of the Commissariat who accompanied him listened to his ludicrously feeble reception of Convict Reynell's attack on the System's amenities.

'Reynell,' he said, stepping a pace nearer to the ranks as he spoke, 'I am going to trust you—I will give you a farm—you and any four others you may choose to pick out of the old hands!'

'You—are—not jollying—me, your Honour?'

'No—you will find by and by that I never "jolly!"'

'Then, by G—, sir, I'll be true man to you!'

From the rank of men from which Reynell had been called out came in two or three distinct voices a shout of—

'The Ring'll see 'bout that! The Oath! The Oath!'

II.

Reynell, instantly flushed with the strenuous hope that had been created by Maconochie's words, paled as instantly. Then—

'I'll take it back, y'r Honour. I'll remain as I am—a "good" man!'

'That's right, that's right, my man!' rejoined the Commandant, genially. Again, a sibilant chorus from the ranks. The transports were tickled agreeably at what they thought his misapprehension. They had understood Reynell. Reynell, they knew, was simply adopting the vocabulary of the damned, in which 'darkness was light and light darkness.' But the laughter stopped instantly as Maconochie raised his hand—and did the fatallest thing of his commandancy.

'Men!' he exclaimed, 'no more of that! And now listen!'

A rubbing and clinking of irons and a shuffling of feet rose on the calm air as the men settled themselves into position. They had heard they had got a 'bad' preaching Commandant—and now Fate was about to confirm the report by cursing them with a second sermon on the one day.

'Men, listen! A threat has been used about the Ring. Now, I tell you—Ring members and nonmembers of the Ring—that I am resolved to crush that society out of existence.'

From among the massed men a confused clamour arose. 'So other Com'dants have said—and they failed!' 'Better not try!' 'Ye'll ha' to croak first!' A chorus of defiance in which rumbled an accent of triumph. The System for three generations of Islanders had been trying to kill the Ring, and the Ring was still immutable and impregnable. The men who were of the Ring feared its despotism, but gloried in its traditions and its power. The men whose names were not scored in its mysteriously-kept roll, respected it and admired it, for was it not a rock that withstood the shocks of the Authorities?—an empire supreme over an empire otherwise omnipotent?

Now, Maconochie had meant to say that the only uprooting force he intended to apply to the Ring was that of kindness and justice. His wish was to render the Secret Society innocuous by depriving it of any occasion for the exercise of its undoubtedly enormous capacity for desperate action. But he was given no chance of explaining himself. Though they thought that the loss of their Sunday dinner—deeply cherished treat!— was involved in the uproar, the one hundred and fifty men, moved by a common impulse of passion, which, like a tornado-wave, swept all before it, continued and increased their clamour. They shouted, whistled, clanked their irons. Every sound was an inflection of evil. To the officials inured by years of familiarity with the Island life to such demonstrations, there was nothing particularly alarming—certainly nothing distressing in the storm. To the Commandant, however, sensitive in feeling, exalted in imagination, and subject to a curious persistence of reasoning which convinced him every transport was less an offender against society than a victim of society's errors and stupidities, the noise was a literal shock.

He held his hand up to command silence. A strong hiss from the centre greeted the gesture.

He folded his arms, as though to wait patiently for the cessation of the tumult. The challenge was responded to by shrieks of laughter.

He lifted his cap and passed his handkerchief across his forehead. Fifty hands derisively copied the action. It was an admission that he was beaten, and they delighted in it as their nostrils would have done in the scent of roast meat.

He turned his back upon the ironed men, and motioned to a gaol-warder.

Assistant-Deputy-Commissary-General Shanks thought he purposed to order up the main-guard, and for the first time was prepared to confess to himself that the Commandant was something more than a dreamer. And—Mr. Shanks was to be disappointed.

Instead of bringing up at the 'double' a file of twelve men—instead of issuing in bloody sequence, incisive commands: 'Ready! Present! Fire!' Captain Maconochie had sent to his own stores for—tobacco! The imbecility of that act!—how it started Mr. Shanks! How it spoilt his Sunday's dinner and compelled him to sacrifice his afternoon nap so that he might write to Governor Gipps and Mr. E. Deas-Thomson!

'Tobacco for rebels! The establishment is going to the devil!' he groaned later to Mrs. Shanks. 'Tobacco!—when they should have had lead. If he had made requisition upon me, and not have drawn from his own store, I'd have refused there and then!' For Mr. Shanks' heart was sore within him.

As for the gentry of the Iron Room, their turbulence held till the box of tobacco was placed at the Commandant's feet. And then it faded, with a final hiss and splatter as a breaking wave dies against the shingle. They were stupefied at this unique form of punishment.

''E's a-goin' to 'eap coals o' fire on our 'eads!' exclaimed some one, but the remark passed unheeded. The mass were too surprised even for ribald comments.

III.

'Reynell!' Maconochie called.

Reynell looked round before answering. Did the Ring raise objection? If it did, there was no visible or audible sign of its refusal. And he stepped forward; and, to the Commandant's pleasure, saluted.

'Reynell, call out four men to assist you!'

'What for, sir?'

'To distribute that tobacco—half a fig to a man.'

Reynell stared at the Captain—then gazed back at the massed men. For guidance—for a hint as to whether he dare take the bride on their behalf? Most likely so. And so near is weak kindness to refined cruelty, there was not one man there in those ranks of ironed, yellow, brown-and-grey garbed felons with the symbols of shame on their bodies and the glare of the human beast in their eyes, but hated Maconochie in that moment of ordeal. Not a man there but would have risked severe penalties to obtain a fraction of a fig; scarcely a score of the one hundred and fifty but what had already gone through the mire of humiliation for a 'bit.' Therefore their hearts beat with a venomous strength—because he tempted them sorely. For why did they not answer to Reynell's unspoken inquiry?

Those who were not of the Ring dare not speak. In collective action the Ring led the 'private' convicts.

And those who were of the Society grew weak with the temptation. But then—to accept it was to acknowledge Maconochie's supremacy, and to confess a defeat.

For half a minute the two parties stood silent. The surf, half a mile away, drove its monotone over the still air. From the wooded sides of Mount Pitt, on the other hand, travelled, not unmelodiously, the screech of parrots. A wedge-tailed eagle poised majestically over the square, and hoarsely flung a taunt to the imprisoned creatures. Save for these sounds, the parade was as silent as is the lull before the revolt of thunder against its confines.

Then—first one sharp 'No!'—next, two or three were joined in the repetition—and finally, in impetuous volume, the fierce negatives rolled from the ranks. Never did monk of the desert make so great a renunciation! In that volleyed monosyllable those outcasts of civilisation refused a pleasure for which, under other circumstances, they would have gleefully bartered their souls.

'No!' A brazen, defiant 'No!' which epitomised the curses of Tophet.

Reynell marched back to his place; and Maconochie knew, as the storm of curses and cheers burst out again, that the Ring was triumphant.

IV.

Unless ——

Commissariat-Officer Shanks suggested, with a semi-sneer, the application of old methods. 'Try, Captain Maconochie, a platoon! There's pretty considerable of a quietening influence in a volley, sir! That is mutiny, and if you don't get the better of them now, they'll have every iron off their ankles in an hour, and then you'll have to shoot the lot, unless you want us all killed.'

'No!' replied the Commandant. 'Ball-cartridge is the last thing I propose to use on society's wrecks. Mr. Gaoler—this thing has gone far enough. Finish the muster and give 'em their dinners!'

'What, sir! Their dinners!' Really, the gaoler was to be excused for his patent astonishment.

'Ay,—the poor fellows shan't suffer for my blunder in tactics. The mistake was mine—I've taken 'em the wrong way to-day.'

And with this remark, so subversive of all the conventions and principles of the System—for whenever before did a penal commandant admit he was in error?—Captain Maconochie touched his cap, in graceful acknowledgement of the salute of his subordinates, and left the muster-yard.

*   *   *

The whole of the Iron Room transports enjoyed their dinners the more for the sauce of triumph. For dessert they were gratified by another delicious morsel.

The Commandant sent an order to the gaoler to despatch by 6.30 a.m. on Monday, Henry Reynell, per *Coquette* (Colonial), and 'four other men that the said prisoner should nominate,' to Farm 5 B, therein to be installed as 'sub-gang in charge.' The proceeding was, it is needless to say, altogether exceptional. But then the Island owned an altogether exceptional commander, and it had proved a day of exceptional occurrences. And it was, doubtless, in accordance with the spirit of the joke that the gaoler, as he communicated the decision to Reynell, mocked him by doffing his cabbage-tree, and addressed him with a scoffing irony.

'Would it please Mr. Reynell to nominate the gentlemen who were to accompany him?'

Reynell took the jest admirably. He craved five minutes to make his selection, and within that time had informed the officer that Osborne,

Peake, Barrington, and 'Swinger' Felix would form his comradeship. For the committee of the Ring had raised no objection. "'Twarn't going out to the farmsteads, Reynell,' said a high ruler of the league—a 'Three'—'that we complain of, but your promise to be a true man! No chap in the fellowship shall go "bad" without permission. It's breaking oath!'

And consent being thus obtained—we translate the 'flash' language habitually employed in Ring business—the choice was, as we have said, made, and 5 B group constituted.

On Monday, when the dormitories turned out at 5.30, the first thing done by the new sub-gang was to present themselves at the 'blacksmith's shop' and have the rivets driven from the bazils.

Felix was last at the low anvil. As the bazil of his left leg fell to the ground he expanded the massive brawniness of his chest with long draughts of tonic morning air; and then clutched Reynell with a wrestler's grasp.

'Why, lad, I be tha' man for ever an' a day. I never 'ud ha' got rid o' them damned clinks but for thee until the day I wed the worms. Felix is tha' man for ever an' a day!'

V.

And now let us gather up the links of the story.

Monday was formal court-day, and, therefore, none of the group saw the Commandant till the evening. Muster had passed over—the mutual responsibility farms were mustered only by their leader, he answering for his group—and the men were busy preparing their 'tea,' and rejoicing in the novel sensation of what was virtual freedom, when the Captain walked up to the hut.

They ceased their preparations and saluted. The spontaneity of the movement was plain, and it thrilled the 'old man's' heart to notice it. Something, he thought, of that voluntary respect for just authority, which is an accompaniment of manhood, had been generated in the men by that one day's liberty, and surely his experiment was about to be justified? He smiled gaily as he returned the salute.

'Now, men,' he said, 'don't mind me! Get on with your tea—I am sure you must need it after all this day in the fields!'

In forty years of the System never had Osborne heard the like. He bent his eyes to the block of stone which did duty as a temporary table, and fumbled with his tin maize-meal dish. The others, with the exception of Peake, were also affected; Reynell to the point of turning his head away so that neither the Captain nor his group-mates should discern the tear that scalded his cheek.

'Men!' continued the Commandant, ever deeper touched by evidences of gratitude than by testimonies of insult, 'I wish you would trust me! I want to be a friend to you—to every man of the 1600 souls in prison here! Come, sirs, forget I'm the Commandant—the "old man." Think of me, for the time being at all events, as *a man*—one who deeply sympathises with your sufferings, and who will only be too glad to alleviate them in every way he can without violating his duty to those who sent him here! Come, what do you say?'

Peake was the first to speak. 'Reynell, y'r Honour, is our leader!' A dogged resistance to any softening influence was easily to be understood from his manner.

'Then, Reynell, speak for yourself at least—for the others if you can.'

The ex-soldier drew his under-lip in, and bit it till blood came, in the severity of the struggle between the Past and the Future that might be. Then he gulped rather than uttered his answer.

'I take back—the insult—of—yesterday, sir. I'll be true man to you—so help me God! And the —— Ring may do its worst.'

Maconochie knew that, come what might—disdain from Privy Councillors and Secretaries of State, cold water from Governors, and sneers and insubordination from smaller officials—yet still he had plucked one soul from the pit. After a few more words of friendly tenor he returned to Government House.

Upon his going, Peake dropped his thin mask of hypocrisy and looked what he was—the child of the devil his father, and the System his mother. Other parentage had he known none. When, as a hunchbacked boy of eight, he first understood a little of the meaning of life, the System was already nourishing him at her breasts. And because of this must we excuse him somewhat.

Peake, when the Captain's steps could not be longer heard, pulled off his waist-strap.

'Hold!' He threw out an end to 'Penman Barrington.' 'Barrington' paled—but grasped the leather.

'Reynell, you sneakin' cull—come here!'

And Reynell, too, obeyed the strange command. He took the other end. The strap was pulled taut. Then Osborne and Felix each laid hold upon it in the centre, standing on either side of it. The four thus formed a cross. Sometimes in the cross of the Ring the hands touched and clasped; but never in the cross of denunciation—as this was.

Three—five—seven times Peake walked round the group, and as he moved he recited the Convict Oath.

At last, he stopped suddenly—at the end of the third repetition.

'Osborne, you're a "Sevener"?'

Osborne, hoarse with suppressed fear, muttered 'Yes.'

'And you're a "Sevener," *accused*?' Reynell was thus addressed. He nodded assent.

'What are you, Bill?'

'A "Niner"!' answered Felix.

'Barrington?'

'A "Fiver"!'

'And I'm a "Three". We're all denominations. All denominations necessary to convene when it's a "Sevener" as is to go up before —— Do any object?'

Silence. Only Reynell shuddered.

'Then, the "Niner" shall bid the "Niners," and the "Sevener" the "Seveners," and the "Fiver" the "Fivers," and the "Three" the "Threes" to Ring lodge on Sabbath next if the "One" ratifies, and the business shall be to try "Sevener" Henry Reynell, for that he played our noble Society false, and promised to be true man to an Establishment officer, and defies the Society! So the Devil help you all!'

And some trembling lips muttered a low 'So the Devil help us!'

Part 2—The Session of Denunciation

I.

The Ring had been convened. A 'session of denunciation' had been called in the manner provided by the traditional statutes of the Society, and Convict Henry Reynell, 'Colonial' transport per *Coquette*, had been duly apprised that on the Sunday following, at three in the afternoon, he was to be charged with having violated the 'laws.' He, an initiate, had defied the Ring; he had told Captain Maconochie that 'he would prove a true man to him;' and this after the Ring had ordered that in season and out of season the new Commandant was to be thwarted—not so much disobeyed as thwarted.

When, within a month of Maconochie's arrival, it had become plain what sort of a man he was, the 'One,' on requisition from the 'Three,' had convened a 'Council of Order,' at which it was enacted that the new Commandant was an 'enemy.'

The business of a 'Council of Order' was to enact 'laws' and adopt 'regulations.' It was the least potential of the three descriptions of Ring gatherings.

The second was that known as the 'Session of Denunciation.' It was convened only when a formal charge was to be laid against some member ('initiate' or 'uninitiate') of the Society, or when some person not of the Society was to be denounced for his treatment of a member.

The third was the 'Conclave of Doom.' At this meeting the fiat went forth for punishment, the executioner was appointed, and—if the doom was a capital one and the victim a member of the Society—the vacancy would be filled up.

The 'Council of Order' could be attended by any member of the Ring—whether he belonged to the initiated twenty-five, or to the uninitiated, 'the novices,' whose number was practically unlimited. It was invariably held during a meal-hour, for then only could a large muster be depended upon.

The 'Session of Denunciation' was attended by the 'circles' only, or as many of them as could be present. It was usually held on the nights of Sundays or holy-days, in the Iron Room. The 'circles' were, as a rule, in irons. 'Clinks' and 'Trumpeters' were rather regarded as Ring insignia. Occasionally it was held in the day-time; Reynell's was to be a day-session.

As for the 'Conclave of Doom,' it was constituted only by the 'One' and the 'Three.' If the 'One' was in gaol, or in such other position that his attendance was impossible, then a majority of the members comprising the circles of 'Three' and 'Five' could proceed with the business. The convening of this culminating assemblage, however, rested absolutely with the 'One.' The 'Three' could not constitute the Doom-session without his consent; and in this circumstance consisted the 'One's' power of veto. The twenty-four men constituting the 'circles' might pass a unanimous vote of 'Death!' or other penalty, and by his simple refusal to convene a Doom-session within the period indicated by the law and custom of the Society—which period, in Maconochie's time, was three months—the presumed victim would go free.

At the Doom-session, the proceedings were, of course, controlled by the 'One'—the Centre.

At the other sessions, the president was one of 'Three' circle, who acted as leader. The 'One' might be present, or he might not, at a 'Council of Order,' or a 'Denunciation;' but, if present, he would not take charge of the assemblage. Such a step would have been tantamount to revealing his identity to the 'Ringers' generally, and would have been a violation of the fundamental law of the Society, which ordered that none but the members of the 'Three' should know who was the 'One.' To have torn away the veil of secrecy which shrouded his personality would have deprived him of his power. The Unknown is always terrible.[3]

From the circle of 'Nine' to the circle of 'Seven;' from the circle of 'Seven' to the 'Five;' from the 'Five' to the 'Three;' from the 'Three;' to the 'One:' so ran the grooves of communication.

What, pertaining to the business or the safety of the Ring, a member of 'Nine' circle heard, it was demanded from him, by his sworn duty to the Society, that he should communicate to his colleagues of his 'circle.' And the circle, or a majority, should decide whether the facts or the suspicions should be passed on to 'Seven' circle.

Reaching the circle of 'Seven,' the intelligence, if the circle by majority so decided, would pass to the 'Five.' In like manner, the 'Fivers' would transmit it to the 'Three;' and so the 'Centre'—the 'One'—would hear of it only after long process of filtration and examination.

At any stage of the routine a 'circle' might send back a 'report' for further evidence and information; or, by refusing to pass it on, veto and quash it. The complaint could not be again made by the lower circle till after the lapse of so many weeks.

Should a matter be first set in motion by an intermediate circle, that circle would communicate the essence of the business to the lower rank, but the latter had no voice in referring it to the final judgment of the 'Centre.' All vetoes were similarly communicated, so that the effect was this: Every initiate member knew the nature of all business which by ultimate

---

[3] The theory of the writer as to the personality of the 'One' will be disclosed in the story which follows, 'The Conclave of Doom.' The question of 'One's' identity baffled Marcus Clarke, and the writer might, therefore, have been excused for attempting an answer; but he will venture to propose a solution.

transmission to 'One' became the concern of the Ring; but *every* member had not a voice in its determination. No initiate could aid in the settlement of a matter originating in a higher circle than his own.

The exceptions to this general law were two. For the denunciation of an initiate member, the consent of the circle lower than his own was necessary, as well as that of his own and the higher ranks. Such cases were considered urgent, and the vote of one member of the lower circle or circles was regarded as sufficing for the whole of that denomination. And a 'Three,' invested with scarcely less awfulness than the 'One,' could act independently of his co-'Threes' by 'One's' authority. It was this latter circumstance which originated the belief amongst many uninitiate Ringers that there was no 'One.' They did not necessarily believe that because the 'Centre' was invisible, therefore he did not exist, but they doubted his existence when they saw that attributes they supposed to attach only to the dreaded 'One' belonged also to the 'Three.'

Doubts, however, of this kind belonged to the uninitiates—or novices. The men of the lesser circles—the 'Nines' and the 'Sevens' and the 'Fives'—knew *of* the 'One,' and the 'Three' *knew* him.

They were sufficient, these degrees of knowledge, for they sustained during long years of maleficent working a dreadful society within an accursed community—an empire of evil within an empire of horror. The character of the System alone did not explain the System. You had to take into account also the Ring, which constantly battled with the System, and frequently defeated though it could not subjugate it.

*   *   *

It could not subjugate the System, but then neither could the System destroy it.

The battle was a drawn one: the Ring ceased to exist as the animating soul of all evil things on the Island, only when the System acknowledged itself defeated by the 'paralysing stroke of circumstance,'[4] and abandoned the spot which, designed by Heaven as an earthly paradise, the Englishman had made into a hell. Yet, one thinks, the result should have been different. There was the might of England behind the System—the majesty of her law, the sanctity of her State religion, the wisdom of her administrators. On the other side, there were—what? Twenty-four felons, and the 'One'! A feeble handful of yellow-and-grey-garbed prisoners, most of them habitually in irons, scarcely one that had not shivered as the curling 'cat' kissed him! Why, the System could have hanged them all any morning and not been put to the slightest inconvenience other than doubling the number of coffin-makers for a week!

Notwithstanding, for fifty years the Ring held its own. Its heads or 'Centres'—the 'Ones'—must have been changed four times at least; the 'circles' were re-organised again and again as death came along, and touched some 'Niner' or 'Sevener,' or 'Fiver' or 'Threer,' on the shoulder, and gave him his passport of freedom; the 'uninitiates' were decimated by shootings and the Battle of the Bloody Bridge, by escapes and hangings. Still, the Ring lived on. And it would have been living to-day had the System survived.

II.

The ceremony of convening had been gone through, as we say, and the 'Centre' had approved of the conclave. So the 'Threes' told the 'Fives,' and the 'Fives' passed the notice on to the 'Sevens,' and 'Sevens' to the 'Nines.' Each 'Niner' controlled a body of 'novices,' and to such of these as, in all likelihood, would be in the exercise-yards on Sunday afternoon, he 'passed the word' for picket and guard duty.

And to one other person was the intimation conveyed that a Ring session was to be assembled. The Commandant was so informed—by a note

---

[4] Mr. Gladstone thus alluded to the cause of the breaking-up of the Island penal establishment.

pushed under his office-door! Young though he was in supreme authority, he was at no loss to understand the significance of the pen-printed letter:

'WE MEET ON SABBATH NEXT, THREE IN THE AFTERNOON, IN THE IRON YARD. YOU ARE INVITED TO BE PRESENT TO CARRY OUT YOUR THREAT OF BREAKING US UP.'

It was the boldest challenge to his rule, and that he should not doubt its authenticity, at the foot of the missive was *stamped* (in candle-smoke) the symbol which formed the official signature of the 'One'—the four concentric circles surrounding the double-triangle over the broad arrow.

*   *   *

Over the broad arrow—that stung Maconochie as it had stung Wright, Fyans, Anderson, Ryan, and every other Commandant who had been similarly challenged. For, interpreted, the signature meant that the Ring was supreme over the System. Let the System order, it would be for the Ring to say whether it should be obeyed.

The Commandant consulted the gaoler and such of the overseers as he had divined were not quite enamoured of the old methods of brute force which he was seeking to supersede with kindness, and showed them the message. None could enlighten him as to what would eventuate at the meeting.

'A Riot?' No; that was unlikely. The Ring had other methods of working than to precipitate an outbreak unless it was thoroughly prepared, and the chances were now against anything of the kind being contemplated.

'Shall I stop it?' Well, his Honour might try, but it would be useless. It would take the whole military force of the Island, and the armed civil guard as well, to break up a Ring meeting; and even then ——

'What?' They would communicate their business all the same, and rob everybody of a night's rest.

'How?' Because the signalling would go on the whole night through. The night-guards could hear the signals distinctly from cell to cell; every

Ringer keeps awake and passes on the signal to his right or left as the case may be, though he might not himself understand the significance of the signal.

'But how could the Ring, some members of which were in the gaol-cells, others in the dormitories, others in the Iron Room, communicate, seeing that the three classes of buildings were separated by yards?' Heaven knows!—and the principal Ringers; nobody else!

'It surprises me!' So it did everybody else, the gaoler said.

'Do you think, Mr. Gaoler, the Ring would consent to my making an experiment?' Perhaps so; how?

'If I wished for an illustration of their facility of communicating, would they grant it?' No doubt; and laugh in his Honour's face while communicating. 'Would his Honour like to see a Ringer?' Every officer nearly knew most of the outside Ringers (the uninitiates)—no secrecy was maintained as to that class of membership—but really those fellows knew next to nothing of the Ring proper. The men who formed the outer circles were known also; but the actual participation of each in the working of the Society, why, that could never be proved.

'Were there many regulations in force against the Ring?' Dozens!

'Any definite attempt at suppression?' Yes; and the Battle of Bloody Bridge was the result.

The Commandant sickened at the reflection that here was a force never taken into account by Right Honourable Secretaries of State and honourable members of the House of Commons, or by Judges and Governors. The System might rule by terror in one direction, and by coarse and licentious favouritism in another, but here was a power that defied the tremendous penal organisation created by British justice and British apathy. Buoyed though he was by his intense belief in the truth of his theory, and inspired by his faith in the essential goodness of human nature, he could not, for the moment, resist the awful doubt which now assailed him as to whether it would not be better to let the System proceed on its old lines. A power that continued its machinations under the eye and in the teeth of Authority, surely the only way to deal with it was to crush it by force! These were his thoughts.

Fortunately, however, for his fame, Maconochie resisted the reaction.

When the Lady of Despair, whose breath fanned him for that instant, had passed him, he felt it would be at least wise to wait and see what Sunday would bring forth. He intended to accept the challenge.

III.

O Day most calm, most bright,

The week were dark but for thy light—

Thy torch doth show the way!

Thus had quoted the Rev. Thomas Taylor in his sermon at morning chapel to the Protestant prisoners. His words had been in praise of Sunday as a day which relieved for them no less than for their more fortunate fellows in other places the labour of the week. Their irons might still clank, but they did not fret and jar so painfully, for the movements were those of rest and change, and were not demanded by task-work. Their hands might still require to describe the salute, but the obligation would be less frequent. And the freedom from labour meant opportunity for reading and thought—for recollection of dear ones far away—for indulgence of bright hopes for the future—and for something of that intercourse with their brother-man which, in its unrestricted and unreprieved fullness, would be the principal delight to be conferred by freedom. Something after this manner spoke the tender-natured chaplain, whose spirits had been greatly invigorated since the advent of the new Commandant.

The chaplain's words had touched not a few hearts and had moistened many eyes. Unlike his predecessor, A——, who was for ever throwing 'The Prodigal Son' at their heads; or Parson Ford, of Hobart Town, who was chiefly solicitous that his hearers should prove the value of his teachings by making a decent ending at the gallows rather than in reformation of their lives, Chaplain Taylor invariably impressed the prisoners by dwelling upon the few bright things of the present, and the brighter things their earthly future might still have in store for them. His tribute to the Sabbath was consequently highly appreciated, and more than one out of the six hundred transports in his congregation determined to spend the rest of the day peacefully—if the Ring would let them. That contingency had to be faced, for the knowledge was now general that it was a 'Lodge Sunday.'

The morning muster after chapel passed off without incident—unlike the previous week's, when Convict Henry Reynell—the same who was now accused *by* the Ring—had, *at* the bidding of that body, refused to accept, for his comrades of the Iron Room, Maconochie's bribe of tobacco. And the mid-day meal, of 16 oz. roast-meat, 12 oz. baked potatoes, and the extra Sunday relish—to them who had not been under punishment for the week—of 4 oz. of wheat and barley bread, was unmarked by a quarrel. When the final 'grace' was said, and the Almighty thanked in mumbling, parroted parodies for the mercies so amply showered upon them, the mass of the men in the yards felt they were, indeed, deserving of the pleasure which was to be theirs that afternoon. Not a single prisoner had been felled to the cobbled floors, and not one had rushed to the warders with a complaint that his cheek had been gashed open because he had been indiscreet enough to object to the theft of his ration. The peace of the beautiful Sabbath-day brooded, dove-like, on the resting throngs.

There were five yards, but we are concerned only with the one on which the Iron Room opened, and the adjacent enclosure. These were the pleasure-grounds of the aristocracy of crime; and the Ring membership was most largely represented in them. A doorway, sometimes closed, but on Sundays usually left open, furnished a means of communication between No. 3 yard and the space devoted to the fettered fraternity. From the elevated sentry-boxes—the 'perches'—at the corners, armed guards watched or patrolled the broad-'leafed' walls. Within the radius of a biscuit-throw, two sentries of the military main-guard moved, this one this way, that one the opposite way, from their post at the entrance of a passage leading to the gaol.

At two o'clock the sentries were relieved, and a careful observer might then have seen that a new interest was taking possession of the throngs in both yards. Those who were reading closed their books, talkers became less in earnest, laughers and jesters—these were not wanting, for some men will laugh in hell—abated their merriment, and others who had been nursing their thoughts in abject solitude, shook off their taciturnity and joined one or other of the many knots. All, seemingly, began to count the time.

At a quarter-past two the sentries changed beats. The movement was noticed by the prisoners.

Fifteen minutes later, the soldiers rechanged. The prisoners knew the half-hour had expired. Without any apparent concord of movement, the men in either yard formed themselves into larger groups.

By the next change of 'Go,' talk had nearly ceased in the two yards. Such laughter and sound of chat as were borne on the breeze were from the other enclosures. And the careful observer aforesaid would perceive that now the movements of the men were taking something of the character of marching and counter-marching. He would have heard no word of command; and yet he should have understood that some supreme will was giving directions, for, in the two yards, though no more than a few men in each could see what was going on in the other, there was a simultaneity of movement and likeness of manoeuvring.

And by three o'clock, as the guards were re-adjusting themselves to their original path, the 140 men in the ironed yard, and the 200 in No. 3, were disposed something in this order.

Close to the north wall in the former enclosure stood two men. At three paces distance from them, so placed that, had a cord been passed through the hands of each to the others, a circle would have been described, of which the first two men would have formed the centre, stood three more transports. At five paces from these last were another five prisoners.

Connect these by a cord, and these five would have surrounded the three. At seven paces, again, from the five transports were a second five, likewise ranged in an imaginary circle order. Nine paces away from this latter five was gathered a group of twenty-two or twenty-three—an outer envelope, as it were, of the inner rings. The mass of the ironed men stood by the south wall—and their faces *towards* it; but a weak line of communication was kept up by a string of pickets extending to this numerous group from the outer circle.

Thus was arranged the Ring in day conclave. The central two men represented the circle of 'Three;' the three, the circle of 'Five;' the first five, the circle of 'Seven;' and the second five, that of 'Nine.' Each circle was separated from its next lower one by as many paces as there were members in the lower circle. And the twenty-two or twenty-three 'uninitiates' were divided by nine paces distance from the 'Nines.' The pickets were recently admitted 'uninitiates.' If the Ring had a message for the convicts in general or for the 'uninitiates' who, for purposes of intimidation, were thrust amongst the transports who had refused or not been permitted to join the Society, it was transmitted by the pickets.

The circles of the Ring, it will be seen, were short of their proper number. It was seldom possible, indeed, to constitute a full Ring at a day conclave. Of the twenty-four men making up the circles, fifteen only were in the ironed yard. Of the rest, five were at the 'mutual responsibility' farm, and four were in the next—No. 3—yard.

In the latter yard, allowing for the smaller number of the Ringers, the arrangement was the same. No 'Threer' was included in this enclosure, but a 'Five,' three 'Nines,' and a dozen uninitiates were ranged at the proper gradations of distance. The convicts unassociated with the Ring were crowded under the south wall, with their faces turned from the Society group. Between the twelve uninitiates and the mass stretched, as in the other yard, a line of pickets.

On the stroke of three o'clock, then, this was the order of array in both enclosures. Save for a cough, a clearing of the throat, a friction in the 'irons,' there was no sound among the transports. The sentries walked to and fro—and looked to their primings. The armed civil guards on the perches quickened their senses, but yet refrained from directly scrutinising the proceedings. They could see every face, and yet no guard had ever been found who could, on a formal demand, identify any leader of the Ring. That is to say, none since Major Anderson's time. A warder then had declared to the Commandant he would swear to a score of the inner circles. And within a week he lay on his bed, a shattered lump of carrion. A thirst for information is not always judicious.

IV.

The soldiers by the gaol-passage exchanged. And at that instant a sharp, curiously-modulated whistle shrilled from the 'Threes' in the ironed yard, and was instantly answered by another whistle from the next yard. 'Lodge' was opened.

A 'Five' broke from his circle, and passed to the group of uininitiates. He paused a second before each man, who stooped and whispered something into his ear. Then, from the uninitiates, he passed successively to the 'Nines,' the 'Sevens,' to his comrades of the 'Five,' and finally, to the 'Threes.' From all he gathered the password save from the representatives of the innermost circles. To them he gave it. During his progress there had been countless slightly noisy movements among the massed transports, yet the tension of feeling was so extreme, that many would have sworn there had occurred no sound except that caused by the clink-clank of the irons.

When the 'Threes' received the approving signal, one—Johnson—began to recite the Ritual; the other—Gooch—to lead off the antiphonal responses. Sometimes both the words of the reciter and the response were in vigorous, resonant English; other passages were partly English and partly in the Ring's own variety of the 'flash' language; sometimes both were in the *argôt*. It is unnecessary to say the secrets of the Ring were conveyed in the last form of speech.

Very solemn the liturgy sounded. If the words were sometimes ribald, there was nothing ribald in the manner of their utterance. Except in a Catholic service, no such respectfulness of tone and decency of demeanour were ever voluntarily exhibited by the transports as in a Ring meeting. Any unseemliness was visited with a punishment the more to be feared that its precise measure was unknown to the culprit till the moment of its infliction, but the solemnity of its proceedings was at once the cause and the effect of the Society's influence. The portions of the Ritual which were recited in the vernacular were resonantly worded specifically for the purpose of impressing such of the convicts not enlisted in the strange companionship who might be in hearing. Singular though the statement may appear, it was the religious character given to its ceremonies that made it the weapon it was in the service of the devil. Appeals to occult powers, the element of mystery in gesture and language, the measured intonation, the employment of symbolism, the frequent invocation of dread punishment upon men who violated their oath—all were calculated to inspire awe of and devotion to the Society that used it.

The temporary leader of the Ring, who was reciting, reached that passage in the blasphemous liturgy:

'Is God an officer of the establishment?'

And the response came solemnly clear, thrice repeated:

'No, God is not an officer of the establishment.'

He passed to the next question:

'Is the Devil an officer of the establishment?'

And received the answer—thrice:

'Yes, the Devil is an officer of the establishment.'

He continued:

'Then do we obey God?'

With clear-cut resonance came the negative—

'No, we do not obey God!'

He propounded the problem framed by souls that are not necessarily corrupt:

'Then whom do we obey?'

And, thrice over, he received for reply the damning perjury which yet was so true an answer:

'The Devil—we obey our Lord the Devil!'

In a corner, by the south wall, a youth of twenty, in irons for a freak, dropped his face on his hands and stifled a sob. He had been trying since sermon-time to fix indelibly on his memory the sweet melody of George Herbert's hymn:

> O Day most calm, most bright,
> The week were dark but for thy light—
> Thy torch doth show the way!

and now that music was jostled from his mind by the demons' Litany.

Johnson had arrived at the 'prayer:'

> Render us, O Satan, always flourishing in thy work, always happy in obeying thy law, thou who art eternal, who art always young, who never lackest worshippers and servants to do thy will, who art always rich, and never forgettest those who place their offerings at thy altar—

when from No. 3 yard came a long, involved whistle: and in the instant following a murmur ran along the line of pickets.

Captain Maconochie had accepted the challenge.

V.

He walked through No. 3 yard unattended. His predecessor had never entered it on a Sunday afternoon without an escort of two soldiers. As he passed he acknowledged pleasantly the few salutes he received, and gave no sign that he noticed the majority of the enclosure's occupants declined to recognise his presence. They were waiting to see what the Ring would do.

And the Ring? Save for that murmur of the pickets the session expressed no consciousness of the visitor. The reciter finished the prayer in an even tone:

> Render unto us the rewards of them who obey thee always and God never.

And then suddenly changing his tone from the key of religious solemnity to a simple announcement, said, 'The Com'dant!'

In the same instant he saluted and smiled—smiled derisively in Captain Maconochie's face, as the latter, appalled at the abominable import of the Ritual's words, stood still, showing his distress very plainly.

'Good heavens, men! Did I hear aright? Did I hear you blaspheming your Maker so dreadfully?'

'Wot, sir?' asked Johnson. 'This is the first degree of a Ring meetin,' y'r know! We but say wot we're tol' to say. It's all in the Ritooal, sir!'

'You are in Ring Lodge now?'

'Yessir! First degree!'

'And you blaspheme like this in all your degrees?' Maconochie stammered and stuttered in his horror.

'Wud yer like to know, sir?'

'Yes.'

'Then that's jest wot yer won't get to know from me, y'r Honour!' replied Johnson, and the retort provoked a roar of laughter, half-timid, half-defiant, from the circle. Sunday or no Sunday the laughers would have been tied to the triangles by any other Commandant for that outrage, but Maconochie, albeit severely tempted, overlooked the insult.

'When do you hold your other degrees?'

'In present session, at wunst—unless yer a-goin' to break us up!' Again the fellow laughed.

'I am not going to break you up to-day—'

'Nor any other time!' exclaimed the leader.

''Ear, 'ear!' seconded some 'Fives' and 'Sevens.'

VI.

'Go on with your Ritual!' said the Commandant, after a pause.

'That's wot we intend to do, yer Honour,' Johnson, with measured insolence, responded. 'An' d'yer mean to stop and 'ear us?'

'I do!'

'I 'opes as yer Honour'll be vastly interested!' And once more the Commandant was compelled to listen to a laugh that was a jibe. He let it go by, like the others.

Then the leader resumed his devil's business, and gave, in the next half-hour, the Captain a lesson as to the ingenuity of felonry that he never forgot. Better versed than any Penal Commandant, before or since (save Price), in the 'flash' slang or thieves' language, he yet scarcely comprehended a word of the many concluding parts of the ceremony brought to his ears.

For, as there were grades in the Ring, there were varieties in its speech. There was the variety understood by all novices as well as initiates—the variety known to 'Nines' and all above—another familiar to 'Sevens' and 'Fives' and 'Threes'—one in which only the 'Fives' and 'Threes' were educated. All these forms of *argôt* were used that afternoon, accordingly as the 'Three' in charge addressed himself to a higher circle or a lower.

And, not content with that patent offence to the Spirit of the System, the Ring perpetrated yet another. It held communication with its gesture-language—when a movement of the limbs or head expressed a number, and the number indicated a word or phrase in its 'initiate' code—and in its dumb-talk and its whistling vocabulary. These two last were provisions for use when the legs were ironed and the hands in 'bracelets.' And of all the 'talk' and signalling, the Commandant understood next to nothing. All he knew was that the proceedings shaped themselves something like those in a court of justice.

There were addresses from the leader 'Three' and his colleagues—slowly and impressively delivered; there were steppings forth from the outer rings of men who evidently gave testimony of some sort with right hand uplifted; and there was a brief and apparently impassioned speech from a 'Seven'—the prisoner's feelings prompted him in his excitement to drop into a phrase of plain English, which he corrected instantly upon being checked by Johnson. And, finally, there was the pronouncement of a verdict. Amidst a grim silence, broken only by the shuffling and rubbing of the second 'Three's' irons as he moved from rank to rank of the Circles to gather the judgment, the decision was come to. The whole mass by the north wall heaved a sigh of relief as Johnson lowered his head to receive the announcement.

By the laws, to *condemn* a 'Nine' a bare majority of all present sufficed; to 'settle' a 'Seven,' an absolute majority of the Circles present or absent was necessary; for a 'Five' or 'Three' was required a majority of his own circle as well as the majority of the lower ranks. Proxies were used for absentees, if the latter knew of the business. Reynell was represented by proxy.

Now, of the fifteen chief Ringers present in this Iron Yard but seven voted for Reynell's condemnation. On that vote he would have been discharged of the accusation, for it required thirteen to convict him. But, as we have said, five (including the accused) were at the 'mutual responsibility' farm, and four were in Yard No. 3 adjacent to the Iron Yard. Two out of the five voted, by proxy, 'guilty,' making nine! Would the other four go the same way?

There was a lull in the 'talk' and dumb show, while 'Threer' Johnson pondered an ingenious—but quite satanic—notion that came into his head. He guessed Maconochie would wish for some indication of the Ring's mysterious power to communicate at long distances. That singular capacity had irritated and defeated his predecessors, and naturally he would think with them on that point, however he might disagree on others. Johnson communicated his notion to his brother 'Three' in a whisper, and the other applauded it. Whereupon, 'Wud yer like to see, y'r Honour,' Johnson questioned very respectfully, ''ow we send messages?'

'Yes!' cried Maconochie. If he could but gain some insight into the Ring's methods he would defeat them, he thought. 'Yes—yes!'

'Then y'r Honour'll give us yer word as a gen'elman that yer won't use the knowledge yer gain wi'out formal information on oath from other parties?'

The Commandant felt he was justified in saying he would not.

'Then, sir, there are four Ringers in nex' yard—standin' by this 'ere north wall. I'll send 'em a message so you can see 'ow it goes, an' if yer like, sir, yer can bring the answer!'

Should he do it? Was it a trap for his dignity? The Captain reflected, and decided to take the risk.

'I will bring the answer!'

'Then, sir, I'm going to send this message!' Johnson clanked to a foot's distance from the Commandant, and lowered his voice: '*Do yer vote as the majority 'ere*? The reply, sir, as yer'll get'll convince yer jest that question and no other's gone through. Now, sir, watch!'

The pickets, we have mentioned, stretched from the cluster of the novices to the south wall. At a sharp word from Johnson, they moved, as quickly as their irons would permit, to continue the line to the gate opening into No. 3.

'Now, sir,' went on Johnson, 'that there message is a-goin' to the end of that line. Yer follow it from man to man. Then, sir, do you, please, join this line to the picket inside No. 3. They will pass the message on, an' yer'll get the reply!'

Anxiously Maconochie watched the procedure. Johnson, in dumb-talk, 'spoke' to a 'Nine;' the fellow passed the message to a novice or 'uninitiate' by a gesture; he, turning, repeated it in their slang to a picket. So it went to the line's end. Each man, as he received it, revolved on his heel, and transmitted it to the next, the Commandant pacing by their side down to the last picket. Some of these novices trembled because of his proximity; others simply grinned; the sentries and armed civil guards, in their amazement, grew more positive than ever that the Commandant was 'looney.'

The Commandant—and the message—entered the next yard. The pickets took it up. Man by man, with repetitions of slang, passed it to the group of uninitiates, and then to the three 'Nines.' Then the solitary 'Five' in that yard received it. Maconochie would have sworn that nothing passed from man to man save a few syllables of gibberish. And yet, within a minute, he had been given the reply.

'Yes, sir!' said the 'Five,' saluting, 'we four here votes with the majority!'

*   *   *

Grieving deeply over this misapplication of ingenuity, and wondering how he should meet it and defeat it, Maconochie walked back to where the leader of the Ring awaited him in silence at his proper station.

'Well, sir?' questioned, as deferentially as one could wish, Johnson.

'The prisoner said the four would vote—'

'How—how?' came in hard-breathed exclamations from among the circles.

'With the majority!' The Commandant finished the sentence.

Some laughed at the news; some laughed at the exquisitely humorous notion of making the Commandant the bearer of the fatal decision; and one man—a 'Niner,' a friend of Reynell—said snarlingly (to his own hurt at a later time), 'Yer've given Reynell over to his doom!'

Indeed he had done so, though in all ignorance. How the doom fell we shall tell you later.

Part 3—The Conclave Of Doom

I.

Night in the Iron Room. The majority of the men we saw in the Ironed Yard on last Sunday, when at the 'Session of Denunciation,' are lodged here. Perhaps a hundred seek the phantasm of repose on the low platforms of its floors; the rest, some forty or fifty, are privileged to slumber in a smaller dormitory adjacent. And, save by the utterly reckless (ever, alas! all too numerous among the ironed men) the privilege of sleeping in the smaller room was highly valued for several reasons, only a few of which, however, dare be stated. The transports there accommodated were the first to be let out in the morning—that was one reason; consequently they enjoyed the earliest use of the towels—this was a second reason. And a third, and even more important one, was that they were not liable to be disturbed after midnight by a Ring conclave. It was one thing to enjoy the solemnity of the Society's proceedings in the daytime; a lodge broke the tedium of the monotony; but it was quite another to lose the superior distraction that came in the shape of sleep, simply because the 'One' and the 'Three' desired to pursue with adequate rite and ceremony their machinations against the System. Sleep, so precious to all, was trebly precious to the 'Black Norfolker.' To the felon denizens of the Iron Room sleep was almost as welcome as his 'twin-brother,' death.

And so, when it became known in the Iron Room the Wednesday evening after the Sunday of Denunciation, that in all likelihood a Ring conclave would be held that midnight, the members of the outer circles and the novices of the Ring, no less than the miscellaneous criminals who were not associated with the Society, were somewhat troubled. The day had been marked by one of those hurricanes which, springing with suddenness from the surface of the Pacific, die as suddenly after spending their tropical rage disastrously upon every object within their scope; and most of the men, having been exposed to its violence, were suffering from bodily exhaustion. Maconochie had excelled himself and desecrated the sacred traditions of the Island by ordering warm tea to be supplied to every man engaged in outdoor employment, and in some cases, indeed, he had granted hot rum, and had, further, shortened the evening muster by withholding 'prayers,' so that the prisoners might seek their blankets the earlier. And now the Commandant's solicitude was to be partially neutralised by the mandate of the 'One.' Yet remonstrance, audible and overt, was never once thought of. Had the cases been reversed and it had been the authorities who had with apparent wantonness interfered with the transports' poor comfort, a disturbance would have arisen that would not have been readily quelled. Almost the solitary remark uttered with reference to the Ring's action was that of a wretch, Sam Ward, who from a certain eccentricity of habit—he was for ever speaking to himself—had been refused the greatly coveted honour of admission to the Circles. When the signal went round that a Conclave was to be held and that their rest would be disturbed, he said—'Ah, well—'tis a pity, Sammy! You're always free when you're asleep, and you're so tired to-night, Sammy, freedom'd be all the sweeter!' Beyond these words, the mandate of the Ring met no impediment.

II.

At six o'clock, when the last padlock clinched its hold on the doors, and the bolts shot in the iron shutters of the two windows, the hundred men ceased communication with the outer world till twelve hours later. So the System judged and ordered.

But at twelve o'clock the Secret Society intervened. A careful grinding of a key in a padlock was followed by an almost noiseless drawing of bolts and the dropping of chains. And then the door the System had closed and virtually sealed was opened by the authority of the Ring. The 'One' entered—followed by Peake, the accuser of Convict Henry Reynell per *Coquette*, the prisoner lying under condemnation of the Ring.

The night's conclave was to pronounce Reynell's doom. You may remember that Reynell had been appointed by Captain Maconochie leader of the 'mutual responsibility' sub-gang attached to 5 B farm, and that Peake had been one of the four hardened, reckless criminals whom Reynell had selected to accompany him. 'Barrington,' an exforger; Osborne, a gentleman who, to his brother felons' surprise, judges resolutely refused to hang—all rules have exceptions—and Bill Felix, a stubborn, country-bred half-brute, were the others of the gang. And you may remember further that Peake had denounced Reynell to the Ring because the latter, an ex-soldier, had been so impressed by Captain Maconochie's unforced kindliness of heart as to defy the Ring and promise 'to be true man' to the Commandant. According to the canons of the Society, Reynell had thereby grievously offended, and at his resulting trial had been condemned, Peake and Osborne alone of his colleagues of the farm voting to remit him to the 'Conclave of Doom.'

On this Wednesday night, then, Reynell's fate was to be decided, and Peake, being a member of the dread innermost circle of the 'Three,' had resolved to be present. There was no difficulty in the way of his attendance. The 'mutual responsibility' gangs were free within limits. By eight o'clock (instead of six as in the dormitories and cells) they turned in. To be out of their hut after that hour was an offence against the Regulations, and a violation of the conditions on which they held the farms. But Mr. Peake reflected that no one would be likely to know of his breach of good faith except those who would not 'peach.' The essence of Maconochie's mutual responsibility plan was that for an offence of one member of a gang all the other members suffered, the idea being that while a man would not be deterred from wrong action by fear of his own punishment, he would be restrained by regard for his fellows. Even over rascals of Peake's stamp this idea held sway, and that lump of moral and physical deformity, under ordinary circumstances, would have gone to the death rather than have brought Reynell under the whip of the authorities. A defiance of the Ring was, however, another matter, the wretch reasoned, and notwithstanding his personal debt to the man he denounced, who had obtained for him freedom from irons and comparative immunity from supervision, his stunted intellect perceived but the one duty of denouncing the fellow who had insulted their noble Society, and of pursuing him, if the 'One' permitted, to the doom. It was for this he was present.

And if you ask how the 'One,' and Peake the 'Three,' obtained access to the Iron Room when the keys were under lock and key in the Superintendent's office, all we can tell you is that there were but few prison-locks the 'One' could not open.

*   *   *

The great chamber, as the chief rulers of the Ring entered it, was curtained in darkness that might be felt. In some of the other dormitories a light was permitted after lock-up, but by virtue of their superior distinction the gentry and nobility of the Iron Room were left without a glimmer.

Undeterred by the darkness, the 'One' and his companion passed from the doorway down the middle of the room, as though they were familiar with every inch of the planking. Nor was it till some moments later that a strong, vivid flash from a bull's-eye lantern shot, meteor-like, from the end furthest from the door. The brilliant beam projected its penetrating stroke through the massy blackness, to the distant corners and along the walls that were decorated only with 'Abstracts of Regulations,' and Forms of Prayer. For a full minute it played on the occupants of the room, and then, apparently satisfying the person who held it that all was right, the light was closed again by the lantern-slide. The mysterious business of the 'Four' might be proceeded with, for there were no eavesdroppers or unauthorised persons near enough to hear.

The bulk of the transports were crowded together in the corners nearest to the doors, with their faces turned to the walls, and between them and the upper end of the room the members of the circles of 'Five,' 'Seven,' and 'Nine' patrolled noiselessly in stockinged feet and 'blanketed irons.'[5]

---

[5] 'Blanketed irons.'—Pieces of blanketing were wrapped round the fetters to prevent noise.

These guards, sentries of a very hell, crossed the room from bed-place to bed-place. Not a soul was asleep; and, save the guards, not a body was in motion.

A short space of twelve paces separated the nearest line of guards—the 'Fives'—from the group of four men who supplied the infernal motive-power to the machinery of the Ring. Thus, as the 'One' and the 'Three' communicated only in their 'cant' or 'flash' dialect, excepting in the rare cases when the subject matter of their deliberation passed beyond its far from narrow vocabulary, the Conclave was held practically in private. Shut in the 'Four' were, by the conditions which exalted them to their 'bad eminence.' The 'One' was masked. It would have been the easiest thing for the transports generally to have discovered his identity. They had but to rush in a body from the lower end of the room, and, overpowering the guards, seize the man who exercised over them an authority less questioned than that of the System. An inclination to such an act, indeed, had more than once been expressed by a more than ordinarily defiant spirit among the outsiders, but it had never found general favour. The mass of convicts felt that the Ring, though occasionally a hard taskmaster, gave them ample compensation for the tribute of obedience it exacted. It furnished material for their cramped imaginations and ambitions to work upon—it supplied an outlet for their sense of natural justice so consistently outraged by the authorities—it checked and thwarted the System—it had revenged many of the System's wrongful acts. Nothing to weaken or endanger the rule of the Ring would ever spring from the transports generally: of that the 'One' and the 'Three' felt quite sure. And so they did not hesitate to exact penances and institute forms which the legally-constituted authorities dare not have imitated save at the risk of rebellion. Had the System sent a masked man into the muster-yard of the ironed men and declared that death should be the lot of the bold villain who tore the mask from the face, a score of hands would have clutched at it. What odds the yard had been turned into an Aceldama, if the System had been defied?

Yet the Ring sent its masked leader, whom nobody but the 'Three' knew, and for the secret of whose identity the System was prepared to pay the price of an absolute pardon, kept all ready signed and sealed in the Commandant's desk: no paltry ticket-of-leave—not even the desirable conditional pardon which conferred liberty within Australian boundaries; but an absolute gift of freedom and a present of money besides to carry the informer 'home' and to start him in a new life—the Ring sent this man into the midst of vassals, and they, burning to know who he was, and tacitly demurring oftentimes to his rule, yet crushed their curiosity and obeyed him. 'The Ring is wonderful!' exclaimed Dr. Ullathorne to Major Anderson, who had just described the Ring (from less information than we have) to the young priest. 'Wonderful, sir!' ejaculated the choleric but conscientious Commandant. 'It's damnably annoying besides being wonderful!'

III.

The masked man knew the 'Three'—Johnson and Gooch, inmates of the Iron Room, and Peake, of 5 B farm gang. Nevertheless, from each he demanded the password of his circle and the sign of his membership of the supreme rank but one. At the word being given in a low murmur that stirred the darkness like a witch's spell, he began the brief Liturgy of the Conclave.

'For whose service do we meet?' asked the 'One.'

'*In the service of the Devil—the Devil our Lord!*' responded the 'Three.'

'But the Devil our Lord is Invisible!'

'*Aye, as invisible as death!*'

'Yet is death visible?'

'*Aye, to those who can see!*'

'Then, is our Lord visible?'

'*Aye, to those who can see!*'

'Then how appeareth he?'

'In thee, O One! O Mighty One! O Thrice Mighty One!'

'Turn thou then, O men of the Circles, men of the mighty Ring, whose meaning is Unity in Infinity, and do homage to thy chief, to the vicegerent of thy Lord! Turn thou! Turn thou!'

The men of the Circles, the noiseless patrol, faced the Conclave, and in the next instant cried as with one voice:

'To thee our Lord Satan do we homage!'

As they cried their hands were upraised. That much could have been observed, for in that same moment a lurid illumination blazed suddenly upon the scene and hung a garland of flame upon the brows of these human demons.

Through the eye-orbits of a human skull apparently suspended in mid-air, through the opened jaws, through the nasal cavities, and from every fragment of the bony box that had once held the secrets of a human brain, grinned a phosphorescent glare. A mere bit of theatrical mummery, it had a diabolic effect upon weakened nerves already prepared by an incantation muttered in the solemn hush of midnight to be sympathetically impressed. It stamped the seal of supernaturalism upon the ceremonial, and in the perversion of moral sense which characterised the 'Black Norfolkers' as it has marked no other community these hundreds of years, it was welcomed with a thrill that had more in keeping with a sensual pleasure than a retributary terror.

IV.

With the fading of the light the Conclave passed into its most secret stage.

The formal report of the voting in the 'Session of Denunciation' was delivered to the 'One' by Johnson, the leader who had presided. And the 'One' required of the 'Three' by their oath to him and the Ring, whether the condemned Henry Reynell had had a fair trial according to the Society's usage?

And two of the 'Three' affirmed that he had. Peake, the third man of the 'Three,' as the accuser, was silent.

'Had the accused been notified that he had been condemned after the trial and in due form?'

Peake affirmed he had borne the message of condemnation 'with truth, without prejudice, without fear, and without favour.' The message had been of necessity sent through Peake, although he was Reynell's prosecutor, because Peake was the 'Threer' having earliest access to the condemned.

'And the condemned! Does he appeal?'

'No. By his oath to the Society, admits he forfeited allegiance by promising to be true man to an Establishment officer, but craves, if the doom be death, one favour.'

'What?'

'That he may not be drowned or strangled, but that having been a soldier, he may be shot or stabbed.'

Then, after a pause, which held possession of this temple of damned souls as does the tragic interval before the *anathema* claim the vast spaces of a cathedral of the Church in the hour of excommunication, the 'One' pronounced the Doom.

'By the power that is mine, by the authority conferred upon one by our dread Society of the Ring, do I issue my fiat to and make order of doom upon Brother Henry Reynell under bond to the Crown, upon the Crown's register No. 37-889 per colonial ship *Coquette*, and upon the roll of the Society for this year current, No. 12 of our Circle of 'Seven.''

'And the Doom is, *That he shall die the death!*'

'*So be it, O One! So be thy fiat obeyed, O Mighty One! So be thy order of Doom completed, O Thrice Mighty One!*' Thus, in their *argôt*, responded the 'Three;' and when their murmur had been swallowed by the silence, the 'One' went on:

'Who, of his brethren of the Ring, stands nearest to the condemned Henry Reyne'l in brotherly affection—to whom is he most dear?'

Quaking, shiveringly, Peake made answer: 'William Felix, under bond to the Crown, and on the Crown's register No. 39-204, on our roll No. 20 of Circle of "Nine," stands nearest to the condemned.'

'Speaketh the deponent truly?'

'The deponent brother speaketh truly within our knowledge,' confirmed the others of the 'Three.'

'Then let the warrant of doom go forth to Brother William Felix, No. 20 of our Circle of "Nine," that he shall do the deed of death within the circling of a moon's orbit upon his brother the condemned by act of shooting or by act of stabbing, though the testimony be true that the condemned is near to him and dear to him—aye, though the condemned be bone of his bone, blood of his blood, flesh of his flesh, let him do the deed, on peril of his suffering like doom. And from this fiat shall there be no appeal, because—'

The 'One' waited for the antiphon. It came solemnly from the 'Three:'

'Our Society has been wounded, and it heals its hurt by blood.'

'So cut we off all traitors! So doom we all that ally themselves to the Law which persecuteth us—the Law which hath given us over to the living death!'

'So cut we off all traitors! So doom we all that ally themselves to our persecutors!'

V.

Then proceeded to its conclusion this mummery. Its rites and ceremonies—the devices of ingenious and fertile minds compelled by Fate to that most Sisyphian of all tortures, the working upon themselves for want of an outlet for their inventive and imaginative faculties; or of souls capable of forging thunderbolts and of venting forked lightnings, but condemned by society to the unrelieved, hopeless misery of petty taskwork—were, as yet, incomplete.

The 'One' had to travesty in blasphemous syllables the prayer commonly used at Norfolk Island executions when a Protestant was to be hanged. The original prayer was this—

> Oh, Almighty God, who according to the magnitude of Thy mercies dost so truly put away the sins of those which truly repent, that Thou rememberest them no more, Open Thine eyes upon this Thy servant who most earnestly desireth pardon and forgiveness. Remember him, most Loving Father; whatsoever hath been declared in him by the fraud and malice of the Devil or by his own carnal wilfulness, do Thou forgive …

The infamous parody of that pathetic appeal as recited by the 'One' dare not be quoted. Invert every petition of the original; substitute the name of the Adversary for that of the Deity; invoke as the cause of the victim's ruin and death the loving-kindness of God and the benignity of British Justice, and you will have a faint idea of the prayer he used. The parody was the richest fruit of the System. Were you to clothe with literary form the mouthings of the creatures led by Hébert, as they danced round Lais and Phryne enthroned as Goddesses of Reason on the desecrated Church altars of Revolutionary Paris, you would scarcely parallel it in point of blasphemous horror.

The recitation ended, the 'One' and 'Three' commended themselves and the Ring to the care of the Lord of Evil, and finally—the Circles being once more bade to do homage—the Convict Oath was chanted in chorus. With foot against foot and palm meeting in palm, the Bond of Obligation was renewed.

Only, there was no drinking of blood from one another's pin-pricked veins. Was it because of the darkness that the libation was omitted? Was it because time was passing?

No; the blood was not drunk because, in the presence of a superior infamy, an inferior shame is superfluous.

A 'Conclave of Doom,' at which was marked the period of some Ringer's life, fulfilled yet another awful function. It at once elected some one to the newly-created vacancy. There were always waiting aspirants for admission to each circle from the grade below it. The man eligible for promotion from the novices or uninitiates was almost invariably in attendance, but if his presence could not be secured—say, because he was in gaol, in Longridge Barracks, or at the Cascades—he was admitted by proxy, the proxy, one of the initiates, being compelled to administer the rite to the newly-elected at the earliest opportunity.

Now, Reynell being a 'Sevener,' the vacancy in 'Seven' Circle had to be filled by the appointment of a 'Niner.'

Felix, the nominated executioner, was chosen. This step followed the usage. The executioner, having at supreme risk obeyed the Ring, was worthy of promotion if the deed of death created a vacancy.

To fill Felix's place and thus complete 'Nine' Circle, a novice was called up by name from the silent, wearied, but docile throng by the door. As the wretch stumbled in the darkness up the length of the uneven boards towards the first line of patrols, his movements were followed by a plaintive wail from Sammy Ward.

'Ain't you going to elect me? It's my turn!' And he was hardly stopped by the smothered exclamations which burst from those equally unprivileged with himself. 'Hush, you fool! hush!'

The newly-honoured convict reached the first patrol. There he was stripped—and passed on.

When he came within arm's reach of the 'Three,' the flash of the bull's-eye blazed into his face, and, for an instant, blinded him. This was done to identify him. Once, two years before, when a man had been called from the outsiders to be graced with his new honours he grew, at the last moment, craven. The man next him whispered that he would go in his stead. He did so, and—up to that night the lantern had not been used for that last flash of identification—was initiated beneath the cloak of darkness. The next day he claimed, as he was entitled to do by his rights of admission, instruction in the 'cant' language from an elder member of the Ring. Then he stood revealed as one who had fraudulently obtained admission to their mysteries. The morning following he was found dead in his bed-place; obviously strangled. 'But what was the use of an inquiry?' questioned the Acting-Commandant Bunbury. 'To hand the murderer we should have had to hang one hundred and twenty men!' So the flash of identification became necessary.

The man passed the scrutiny—he was the right one, the one who had been called and chosen, and he was initiated.

Gagged in the moment when the light blazed in his face, he could but writhe in the grasp of two 'Fivers,' and utter throat noises as the 'One' thrust a hand against his chest, and punctured its skin with, it seemed, a hundred needle-points. In the shock of pain the neophyte scarcely knew what followed. Into the hundreds of minute wounds, as soon as the needles had been withdrawn, was rubbed a handful of gunpowder. When healed, the scar would describe a solitary circle. Thus was the symbol of the 'Niners' impressed upon its new member.

The impression of the symbol was, however, only the first part of the ceremony of initiation. What completed it may not be described, nor even hinted.

 Suffice it to say that if by any lucky chance—it was all a business of pure chance—the neophyte had not to the moment of his initiation into the Ring committed any *capital* offence, the completion of the ceremony placed the rope round his neck. Every member of the Ring was, by virtue of his membership, liable to be hanged. It was really an organisation of the condemned. And so absolute was the moral ruin of 'Black Norfolkers,' that that terrible fact was considered the most brilliant trophy wrested by the Secret Society from the Law.

VI.

It was three in the morning before Peake reached the hut on 5 B farm. His hut-mates—Reynell, Osborne, 'Barrington,' and Felix—were waiting for him in a weird, Rembrandtesque half-light—waiting for the news of the doom. In his walk from the Iron Room to the farm he had passed three sentry-posts; but the 'One' had given the countersign at each, and the quiver of trepidation with which Peake had come within range of each soldier's musket had proved quite unnecessary.

Not so, perhaps, the spasm which shook him when he re-entered the hut. The exhilaration of the ceremony had evaporated, and his sense of duty to the Ring was overlain by his awakened remorse that he had betrayed to the death the man who had become surety for his good conduct, and had thereby obtained for him comparative freedom. From the remorse sprang the dread that Reynell—already on his way to the grave—might avenge his betrayal on the betrayer. What would Reynell do?

For some moments after Peake entered no one spoke. Then the condemned broke silence.

'Is it—doom, Peake?' he asked.

Peake nodded.

'Who,' stammeringly questioned Osborne, 'who is the Ketch?'

Peake, with a trembling forefinger, pointed to Felix.

Felix, great hulking lout, bent himself in the shadows, and covered his face with his gnarled hands.

'An' I'ad promised to be true man for ever an' a day, 'Arry! Yo brought me here, 'Arry, an' rid me o' the domned clinks, an' it's me that's to kill tho. I'udn't do it!' He half said, half groaned these words.

'Then, if yer don't, it's yer doom too, yer know!' breathed Osborne.

'An' I'd take it 'fore I'd break my oath to 'Arry yonder. I'm his sworn man.'

'Yer the Ring's man first!' insisted Osborne.

'Ay, that war I; but there's a way to obey th' Ring an' keep my oath to 'Arry too!'

VII.

On the morrow—rather, at a late hour the same day—while the sub-gang were absent at maize-hoeing, *an Establishment officer* visited the hut. Save him, no man entered the hut between the time of the gangers leaving it and their return. Yet when they came back for their noon-tide food, one and all of them—fellows who would have laughed at death had it come from Law and the authorities—changed colour as they saw on the stone table a scrap of folded paper.

On the outside of the paper was inscribed a single circle, with the figures '20' in its centre.

On the inside there was no word; only there were inscribed two circles, so—

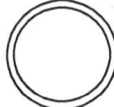

In the common centre of these was the roll-number of Henry Reynell— 'No. 12.'

And below this symbol of the personality of the condemned was, stamped in candle-smoke, this—

It was the 'One's' signature to his order of doom upon Henry Reynell, 'No. 12' of Circle 'Seven,' and the warrant was addressed to 'No. 20' of

Circle 'Nine'—William Felix. It was his roll-symbol which was marked on the outside of the paper.[6]

*   *   *

How Felix obeyed the warrant, and yet kept faithful to his vow to be sworn man to Reynell, will be told presently.

Part 4—The Falling Of The Doom

I.

The Secret Society of the Ring had, in regular conclave, ordered that Brother William Felix, No. 20, of 'Nine' Circle, should, within one lunar month, stab or shoot to the death Brother Henry Reynell, No. 12, of 'Seven' Circle. Reynell's offence was (as already related) the promising 'to be true man' to Civil Commandant Maconochie. Convict Bill Felix was a member of the sub-gang of which Convict Henry Reynell was the leader; and, inasmuch as Reynell had chosen Felix to be a member of 5 B farm sub-gang, thus freeing him from the constant wearing of fetters and conferring upon him a desirable degree of freedom, Felix had sworn to be his (Reynell's) man 'for ever and a day.' The tie of fraternity which linked Reynell and Felix thus was sadly complicated with the obligation of obedience which bound the latter to the Ring. Let Felix obey the Ring, and he would have to enact the doom upon the one soul for whom he cared. Let him refuse to execute the death-warrant issued under the seal of the 'One'—the dread head or 'Centre' of the Society—and the doom he refused to Reynell would be his own. The Ring having given over some one to the doom, would demand the life of the appointed executioner if

<hr>

[6] For these illustrations of the symbolism of the Ring—indeed, for almost the whole of his knowledge of the Secret Society's ritual and ceremonial—the writer is indebted to a venerable (using the word in its literal sense) man, who, though an ex-'Norfolker,' was an esteemed correspondent of the late Dr. Ullathorne, R.C. Archbishop of Birmingham.

he failed within the specified time to complete his task. In rare instances a regulation or law of the Society might be modified or altered in effect. But never in its history had there been known a case where a death-warrant had been left unfulfilled and the stated executioner had continued to live. The idol would demand appeasement for its lust, if not in the person of one victim, in another's.

There is an impressive story as to the working of this Medean law. Before the existing 'One' it is believed three men had filled the awful office. The second in the administration had been ordered to murder the then Commandant, Captain Wright. He had acquiesced in the need for the crime—otherwise the order would not have been ratified. And, as the 'One,' it was his duty to perform the doom on the Commandant. It was a minor but still immutable law of the Ring that the 'old man' should only die by the 'One's' hands. The honour was accorded to him as a privilege of his dignity. Yet Captain Wright lived to be Major and to give evidence before the Select Committee on Transportation of the House of Commons. How was that?

Wright had been suddenly recalled to Sydney. The vessel which brought the summons of recall could not lie off the harbourless island in the storm-season for longer than a week, and instant preparations for his departure were set on foot by the Commandant. The news spread—and twice within the week was his life attempted in vain. He got on board the vessel safe; thus unknowingly he committed the 'One' to the wrath and vengeance of the Ring; and the Ring demanded its vicarious sacrifice.

Three days after Wright's sailing the body of one of the most intelligent of the 'free' constables was found suspended from a tall pine. The dead man was supposed to have been in pretty general favour with the transports and his fellow-officers; hence it was not believed that he had been murdered, and his death was attributed to suicide. The military surgeon, who made an examination of the corpse, drew the attention of the subaltern of the guard to a curious symbol burnt or tattooed into the flesh of the chest and freshly cut across with a knife. The scarification was, however, only skin-deep, and had been done after death. The officers did not recognise at the moment the significance of the scar.[7]

It was the symbol of the 'One.'

Not even the dreaded Head of the Society was free of its penalties.

II.

Civil Commandant Maconochie, it will be remembered, had, in his anxiety to acquire a knowledge of the Ring's methods of communication, been trapped into conveying the report of how certain Ringers had voted at the trial of Reynell. 'Condemnation or Acquittal?'—the question hung thus in the balance when Maconochie had appeared in the yard where the Ring Lodge was in 'Session of Denunciation.' Nine were for condemnation—for sending on the accused to the 'Conclave of Doom;' but thirteen votes were required by the law of the Secret Society before the condemnation could be passed. And four votes Maconochie had been trapped into conveying.

---

[7] It is supposed that the incident here related was the origin of an order once issued by John Price by which every 'bond' and 'free' constable was required to present himself stripped for examination by a medical officer at certain periods. The 'bond' constables had no alternative but obedience, but the 'free' officers, almost to a man, refused to submit to periodical inspection as degrading. They appealed to the Governor in Van Diemen's Land, who upheld the objection, in their case, 'till Mr. Price could show specific reason for the proposed course in the interests of discipline.' Price replied in (for him) a remarkably indiscreet manner—in what was known as a 'Semi-official communication'—by alleging that it was necessary to find out from time to time 'whether officers' personal marks varied.' Thereupon Mr. Price received one of the few snubs of his official career.

Without knowing the precise bearings of his action, he had learnt enough to understand that he had given Reynell over to the doom. An interjection by a Ringer who was a loyal friend to Reynell—strange, how in this accursed community of felonry, which a noble member of the House of Lords stated to be deficient in every human attribute, feelings of affection refused to absolutely die out, and thus prove his lordship right!—had informed Maconochie of so much. What was the doom: death, mutilation, or a simple 'sending to Coventry'? Maconochie asked several of the officers of the Establishment, but could gain no satisfactory answer. 'Most likely death!' he was told by the gaoler. 'The Ring didn't think much o' death!'

Herein the gaoler was subject to that tendency to error which infected all thoughts and beliefs, of whatever nature, held in the University of Depravity.[8] The Ring thought a good deal of death when that Mighty Leveller was enlisted on their behalf. It was only when Death acted for the authorities that they snapped their fingers in his face and jested pleasantly with him. When the Ring used him, he was to its members an instrument of terror, and they surrounded him in their imaginations with every ghastly, every agonising, every horrific attribute of which the distorted culture of the Society's founders, or the dark fancies of the most ignorant Ringers—such as those who ever trembled at the verge of madness—could invent and adapt. But, so momentous is the alteration in human feeling, which can be effected by changing the point of view, Death had but to draw his fees from the Establishment to be sneered at, ridiculed, and derisively welcomed. Black Norfolkers went sardonically to the grave at the Establishment's orders, just because the Establishment wished them to do differently.

III.

Maconochie sent for Johnson, leader at the 'Session of Denunciation.'

---

[8] 'University of Depravity.'—Archbishop Whately, in his speech to the House of Lords, of May 1840, on his motion for the abolition of Transportation, thus described Norfolk Island.

'Have you any objection, sir, to relate the precise significance of the condemnation which you understand the Ring has passed on prisoner Reynell?'

''Eaps!' was the laconic rejoinder.

'I beg your pardon! What did you say?'

''Eaps! I sed I 'av 'eaps of objecshuns.'

'Oh!' Then, after a pause, 'I believe, Johnson, you have been a prisoner under the Crown for many years?'

'More'n can count!'

'Yes? Then you must have heard read many times the regulation as to answering truly and explicitly, and without prevarication or evasion or denial, all questions put by persons in properly-constituted authority?'

'Can't say as I 'av, yer Honour!'

'Johnson!'

'Yes, yer Honour?'

'I mean to deal fairly and kindly with every man on the Island—but I will have truth-speaking. I never forgive a lie, except it is uttered under the influence of terror!'

'In wot 'av I lied, yer Honour?'

'You said you had never heard the regulation enforcing—'

'Savin' yer Honour's presence, I said nothink o' the kind! Yer arsked me 'ad I 'erd it read. Well, I never did! I've 'erd it mumbled ev'ry Sunday since I was a kinchin—but never 'erd it read wunst. There ain't no 'Stablishment orf'cer as can read—unless it's yerself.' The rascal grinned in enjoyment of his own satire.

'You know the meaning of the regulation—what it enforces—however?'

'O'course: to answer th' truth, th' 'ole truth, an' nothink but th' truth w'en 'terrogated by 'Stablishment orf'cer.'

'Then answer me, sir.' (Not imperatively, but with a studied politeness, did Maconochie now speak.) 'What judgment—what 'doom' as you call it—has your Society ordered upon Reynell?'

Johnson gazed reflectively at the ceiling. He passed his right hand over the corrugations of his forehead, and drew it down the scarred and weather-blighted cheeks to the stern, square jowl that had gripped numberless groans of agony in their utterance, and bid them be dumb. Then he said:

'Mr. Com'dant, Pa'son Taylor tells us that w'en th' higher law conflicts wi' th' lower, we must allus obey th' higher—allus th' higher. Do th' pa'son's views meet wi' yer approval, sir?'

The Commandant, already once trapped by Johnson, was dubious of the fair seeming of the interrogation, and declined to answer directly.

'Answer my question!'

'Wi' orl respecks, y'r Honour, I can't till I know wot to obey—that as is th' higher law or that as is th' lower!'

'There is no question of higher or lower law here, my man—none. It is merely a matter of answering my question. What is Reynell's doom?'

'That's w'ere yer an' me jest differ, y'r Honour. 'Tis orl a matter o' higher an' lower law. If I answer th' question, I obey th' law o' th' System. If I don't answer it, then I obey th' law o' th' Ring, an' I'd 'av y'r Honour know as fur me an' sech as me 'tis th' Ring's law as is highest law.'

Again the fellow's lips parted and his cheeks wrinkled in a gleeful defiance of authority.

'You're talking foolishly,' rejoined the Commandant, bearing the implied taunt with a patience of tone and manner that, if he had only known it, was more likely to penetrate to Johnson's better nature than any number of authority-phrased words; 'you're twisting Mr. Taylor's sayings to suit your own purpose. Mr. Taylor meant, no doubt, that when human law conflicts with the moral law of conscience or revealed law, then the latter, as the higher law, must be obeyed.'

No more unfortunate admission could have been made by a System's officer; and the ingenious Johnson, whose naturally sharp wits the attrition of adversity had ground to remarkable keenness, while wearing away the moral part of him, eagerly seized the opportunity thus offered of making an embarrassing criticism on the System.

'That's jest it, y'r Honour—that's th' very identical thing as I mean. Now, th' System's laws an' reg'lashuns is th' lower law, an' our laws an' reg'lashuns—th' Ring's laws, that is—they're th' higher, 'cos—But will yer 'ear th' reason, yer Honour?'

'Go on—though you are talking insubordinate nonsense. I will hear what you have to say!'

'This is th' reason. Th' Ring's law is th' moral law 'cos it's founded on justice!' He stooped, and, placing his hands on his knees, crooked his head so as to glare impishly into the Commandant's face to watch the effect of his words, or rather of those he left unsaid.

For not what the wretch said but what he left unsaid stung the Commandant. The implication was clear. The System was not founded upon justice. And in his heart of hearts Maconochie knew the accusation was true. Penalties British law justly provided for those who offended against it, but then British law proposed only to punish, and not to give over the offenders to 'unusual punishment' and utter corruption. The System did this, however—and the taunt went home. But, what could Maconochie do? Argument imperilled his authority, and, after all, *he* did not invent the System. So—

'You decline to answer what is Reynell's doom?'

'Aye, y'r Honour, 'cos th' Ring forbids me!'

'You know I can inflict penalties upon you for refusing to answer my plain interrogatory?'

'Short o' puttin' me into an 'oss' necklace, yer can, sir. But yer won't punish me!'

'Why?' Against his judgment, the Commandant put the inquiry. Similar remarks had been made to him before by men up for punishment, but invariably they had been uttered in suppliant or cringing tones. This fellow, however, spoke with the confidence of knowledge.

'W'y? 'Cos yer know wot I ses is true. An' 'cos, although yer an orf'cer o' th' Systum, yer 'art ain't in the Systum's way o' doin' things. That's w'y, sir. Yer ain't been long 'nuff 'ere to 'a changed th' 'art o' a man fur th' 'art o' a beast. Yer know who said that, y'r Honour?'

Maconochie nodded.

'Yes, o' course yer do. It struck th' 'ol man, 'im as was jest a-chuckin' o' us into Jack Ketch's mouth like so many sweeties—lor, 'e did love to keep th' carpenters an' gravediggers a-goin,' did Billy Burton!—it struck even him orl o' a 'eap! But 'e was wrong 'bout it—an' so is Taylor, an' so are yer, an' everybody else as 'erd o' wot poor Kavenagh said!'

'Wrong—how do you mean?'

'Wot did Kavenagh say? "When I landed 'ere I 'ad th' 'art o' a man, but yer 'av plucked it out an' planted a brute's 'art instead!" That's wot he ses, an' th' jedge an' everybody thinks it's true o' th' pris'ners only. But, man'—he gathered breath to hurl at Maconochie, with greater emphasis, a bitter conclusion—'them words war truer o' th' 'Stablishment orf'cers. Th' System finds orl its orf'cers men, an' leaves 'em orl brutes! Orl o' we don't get 'ardened, but there ain't one o' *yer* wot doesn't!'

IV.

Foiled by Johnson in his attempt to discover the fate in store for Reynell, Maconochie met with no more success when he interrogated the members of the farm sub-gang to which Reynell and Felix belonged. Peake, Osborne, and 'Barrington' each frankly enough declared he knew quite well about the order of doom, but as for telling his Honour—well, the Ring wouldn't allow him.

'If anything happens to Reynell, I shall charge you as an accessory,' said the Commandant to each. And the threat was laughed at. Better the vengeance of the System than the vengeance of the Ring. The former could only hang them—the latter could do more: it could kill them after a ceremony of execration. They were frightened of the last.

From Felix the Commandant received his one fragment of consolation. 'I be 'Arry Reynell's sworn man, y'r Honour! An' no harm 'ud 'appen unto him if Bill Felix can stop ut wi' life nor limb.' And, somewhat reassured, Captain Maconochie went then to Reynell himself.

The man was hoeing. He had stopped for a moment to rest, and stood gazing towards the sea and over the township, which was semi-veiled in a lustrous mist, as though Nature would hide from the eye of Heaven the halls where the devil and the System held their joint revels. On the soft earth the Commandant's steps were inaudible, and the transport did not know of the official's approach till he was addressed.

'Reynell!'

The convict started, and turned round. He 'capped' instantly, and, in the same gesture, Maconochie saw that he had dashed away a tear from his eyes.

'Good-morning, Reynell! The gang making satisfactory work?'

'Yes, sir. I think so! With a fair crop, the Com'sariat'll have to pay them a good many marks.'[9]

Them—why not 'us'? Maconochie was quick to notice the substitution of the word.

'Why "them," Reynell? Why don't you, who are the leader and director of the gang, join yourself with the others?'

'Oh,' with a marked hesitation, and a quivering of the lips that told of an inward agitation, ''twas a slip, sir!'

---

[9] 'Marks.'—Any surplus crop over the rental paid to the Establishment by the mutual-responsibility gangs for their farms was bought, in Maconochie's system, by the Government, and paid for in marks. The marks went towards the purchase of absolute or conditional freedom.

Maconochie stepped forward and laid a hand, with kindly pressure, on the transport's shoulder.

'No, Reynell, it was no slip! It meant that already you are separating yourself in thought from your fellow-gangers—it meant that you are under doom of death from the Ring!'

The condemned flamed out into sudden anger. Such strange tricks does the fancy play with a certain order of superstitious minds, that he was jealous that the secret of the Society he thought so much of as to submit himself quietly to its fatal will, should be thus known to an outsider, and that outsider one of the accursed Establishment. 'Who told you that?'

'No one. I inferred it—partly from what passed last Sunday—you heard I was present?—and partly from what you say was a 'slip.' Come, Reynell— *Harry*—'

All the patience, all the forbearance, all the tenderness that it was possible for one man—a superior—to extend to his inferior, Maconochie caused to vibrate in his voice. The prisoner, bringing himself in the sudden impulse of surprise to face the Commandant, showed in the workings of his features how the 'Harry' had stirred him.

'Tell me,' Maconochie went on, 'if not the doom, how I can help you to escape it. Remember, my friend, that I brought this on you!'

'No!' In a low, choking guttural.

'Oh, but yes! I cannot forget that it was because you swore to be a true man to me, and thereby helped me nobly in what I regard as my mission here, that you are under the ban of the Ring. Therefore, as through me you broke, it would appear, the Society's law, it is only right that through me aid shall come to you.'

'There can—be no—aid, sir! All's up!' Reynell let his head fall on his chest. The action was that of a tired man, of an over-wearied bearer of a burden; there was nothing abject in it.

'No. I pledge you my word, Reynell, that I will get you out of this trouble.'

''Tis no trouble, sir!'

'Listen, sir! I brought you into this quarrel with the Ring because I wanted—well, I wished to count you as one of the trophies of my new methods—'

'Beggin' your pardon for interruptin' y'r Honour, an' it's good of you to put it that way, but it's not true—an' it's no use! I'm doomed—doomed!' And then, with something of that saucy contempt for life which had made him before Maconochie's advent a centre of insubordination, he went on: 'It's not that I'm afraid of death—not a bit of it! No Ringer is—few of us are!' He waved his hand so as to embrace in its sweep the whole group of Kingston buildings—the dormitories, the gaol, and the exercise and work yards. 'None of us are! But no one likes death at the hands of the Ring, for it's disgrace—and besides—'

'What?'

'Yer won't think me a softy, sir, will yer, for saying it? but I've of'n thought of late—' Again he paused, stumbling for an expression. Maconochie waited.

'I've thought that, p'r'aps, life wouldn't be such a bad thing—if one only had—a chance to keep square!'

Maconochie's heart leapt within him. Here was proof that he was in the right! Bring a creature, however hardened to all seeming, within the circle of human interests and brotherly charities; re-clothe him with manhood and individuality; refuse to treat him longer as a mere Number, as a Thing to occupy a line in returns, as an Object of offence to the Law, and, therefore, to have his badness whipped out of him by the Law's agents; let the unforced music of a kind word sound in his ears; do these, and the fountains of a vigorous life would burst impetuously and imperiously from the core of his nature. This was his theory—here was the successful application of it!

He clasped the transport's hand. 'You're right, Reynell—you're right, Harry! Life is worth living—the struggle to make yourself a better man will make it so to you! I'll help you all I can, by removing you out of the reach of pressure from the Ring—'

'You're very good, sir,' muttered the convict, 'but it's too late!'

'It's never too late to repair the past, Harry!'

'Yes, 'tis—in my case. For—look here, sir—can I trust yer Honour—yer Honour's *honour* to keep this secret what I'm about to tell ye?'

'If you insist upon it—yes!'

'I do—I do! Why 'tis too late is this—if I don't die, the chap who's to settle me will. That's Ring law!'

'Reynell!'

''Tis gospel true, sir! An' that's why I've got to bear the doom!'

'I will send you up to Phillip Island yonder till the brig arrives, and then I will despatch you to Sydney,' Maconochie said, confronted with this new revelation of the Ring's potency.

'No use, sir. If I don't die, the chap'll who's to settle me. An' besides, they'd reach me there!'

'I will take you into my household and give you a special guard!'

'The cooks'd poison my rations!'

'I'll send you food from my own table!'

'To reach me they'd poison you and your family.'

'Are they devils?' burst out the Commandant, losing self-restraint for the moment.

'Aye, they are that! But who made'em so—who made *us* so?—for I'm one o'them, sir. The System!' And then, after a pause, while Maconochie rocked himself on his heels in acute distress at these ever-recurring assaults upon the administration of which he was the head, he resumed:

'No, y'r Honour; I joined the Ring wi' my eyes open. I was eager to make a break in my life—it was all work an' punishment, an' sleep, an'devilry, an' then devilry, an' sleep, an' punishment an' work over again—an' the Ring makes a change. An' I'm not goin' beyond Ring custom, especially as my breakin' away would let another chap in for the doom.'

'Tell me who he is, and I'll send him away too!'

Reynell laughed. 'You don't know the Ring, Captain Maconochie! Twenty years off, if that chap's a true Ringer an' met me, he'd do for me then! No, sir, let it be. P'r'aps I'm better dead than alive. I can't do any more harm dead!'

V.

Maconochie, with the taste of ashes in his mouth, left the farm, but instantly despatched an overseer with an escort of a sergeant and four men, and had Reynell locked in a cell, pending his despatch to Phillip Island, where it was his intention to send him. As the escort passed into Pine-lane—a pine-framed avenue leading from the Settlement to Long-ridge—Bill Felix met them as he was on his way to the hut. As he stood aside and saluted the overseer, he glanced inquiringly at the prisoner. Reynell read the glance, and in the Ring language assured Felix to be under no alarm. 'If Felix could not execute the order of doom before the twenty-eighth day (a fortnight had still to elapse), he, the condemned, would perform the "cross-road trick."' Which was—suicide. The Ring should be obeyed; the idol should not be disappointed of its victim.

*　　　*　　　*

A week passed. Under the supervision of two soldiers—one for day and the other for night duty—Reynell was lodged in the solitary hut on Phillip Island. And Bill Felix, appointed executioner, knew that his own—or Reynell's—time was drawing near. Peake, Osborne, and 'Barrington'— none had spoken to him of the imminent event; to have done so would have violated a regulation of the Society; and yet he knew it was an hourly question with them as to the manner in which he would perform the doom. He smiled to himself at the way he would obey the Ring while disappointing it.

Several more days passed. Maconochie himself was on the alert with his telescope at seven o'clock in the morning and five in the afternoon when the sentry on Phillip Island would fire off his musket and thus give the 'all's well' signal. Although the distance between Norfolk and Phillip was but two miles and a furlong, the surf fringing either island made the boat-passage dangerous, and as the Commandant did not feel justified in despatching a boat to the rock save on every third day, he had arranged the gun-fire signal. The report could not be heard, but with a spy-glass the flash could be seen. Flag signals from Phillip's had been discontinued since they had been worked by convicts to destroy a boat's crew.

For seven days the report-speaking musket was fired morning and evening, and Maconochie felt hopeful. He had got it into his head, in spite of what he had learnt, that if the month would pass without the violent death of either Reynell or some other prominent villain being reported, the doom would pass also. And to-morrow would end his suspense. He would send a boat over in the morning.

But on the morrow he himself missed the observation of the musket-fire. He was busy investigating the cause of death of William Felix, No. 39-204 per *Coromandel*, shot dead by the sentry at the outer gaol-tower.

VI.

Bill Felix, with no room in his head for two ideas at one and the same time, had been at first strangely confused by the conflict of the obligations to which he had subjected himself. The Ring held by grips of steel which would not relax, and yet his vow to Reynell tugged at his heart. Reynell had chosen him, Felix, from among seven score of men in irons, and had freed him from 'them domned clinks,' which, encircling his ankles, bit with their subtle corrosion also into his vitals. Most prisoners chafed physically under the compression of the irons; but others—and curiously enough these were not exclusively the naturally refined class—fretted savagely under it both in body and soul. Men who, before exile, had spent their existence for the most part out of doors, in the delicious enfranchisement of wild nature—men who had been shepherds and farm labourers, poachers and gamekeepers, gipsies of the land, or those gipsies of the sea, the merchant-sailors—were fettered doubly. And ex-farm hand

Felix—'an incendiary monster,' Sir William Follett called him at Manchester Assizes—who had been one of a crowd which burnt a farmer's ricks, and who had as much evil in his nature *before* transportation as he had intellect, refused to love his chains. They tortured and burnt him. 'Oh, Mister,' he had said to Major Ryan, Maconochie's predecessor, 'tak' th' domned clinks off, an' yo can flog me week in an' week out, an' yo 'ud!' What Commandant Ryan had refused to do, Transport Reynell had virtually done. Therefore, with the best elements of him, he thanked Reynell—adored him—was prepared to sacrifice himself for him. And in his case, as in most others, affection cleared the wits, and enabled him to perceive the paramount duty.

To the Ring he was bound by respect, fear, terror. To the condemned, he, the executioner of the Ring, was linked by love and gratitude. During that four weeks' reprieve, the debate went on between his poor, dulled brain and his quickened heart. And as the day of doom drew near, so did his apprehension of how he should satisfy the doom become the more distinct. At last he saw his course of action.

It was midnight on the last night but one. Within twenty-four hours must the doom fall, or he himself be condemned and for ever accursed in the annals of the Ring. As he rose from his bunk in the hut on 5 B farmstead he quivered superstitiously in the ghostly darkness. The moon was not yet up; and he had a long—oh, so long a way to go in the myriad-shaped blackness of the night. 'An' he war terr'ble afeard o' th' neet!'

'Be you sleepin', Peake?' he whispered to the hut-mate who slept on the same side as himself.

'No!'

'I be—off—t' do ut, Peake!'

'That's a good cove, Bill, an' ye shall come up higher in the Ring quicker for it!'

Was it fancy alone that thrilled Peake's ears with the words, 'Gord forbid!' or did Felix really breathe them? The scoundrel fell asleep again while trying to solve the problem as to whether his hearing had deceived him.

VII.

Along the pine-bordered lane—a tunnel to hold in the bleak blasts—passed Bill Felix. Gibbering shapes walked with him, 't'owd squoire an' pa'son, an' mither an' feyther from th' whoam village,' and dead and gone brother Ringers, and at least one of the three constables to whose death he had been an accessory. They shrieked at him in the gusts that shook the branches of the tall pyramidal pines, and he heard their sobs plainly in the sound of the sullen surf. He could have sworn some of them laid hold upon him; and great drops of perspiration beaded his forehead and soaked his peakless cap. The wonder was that he did not turn back in sheer affright. But the blind mute impulse which not rarely wins men to heroism when their wills bid them act the coward, held him to his path.

By Government House, the sentinel's shadow silhouetted by the door-lamp on the white garden-wall as he stood in front of the thirty-two-pound gun on the slope, startled him afresh. 'O Gord!' he gasped. He had forgotten that by his oath to the Ring he should have called on Satan.

Past the Deputy-Assistant-Commissariat-General's cottage he stumbled, the scents of rose-tree, spice-plant, and magnolia from the carefully-tended garden banishing for a second some of his dread. He would have liked to have plucked a banana to refresh his parched lips, but dare not jump the fence. He did not want a bullet before his time.

Over the culvert by the Commissariat offices, creeping down by the low wall fearful that the soldier posted there might see him cross the fanshaped beam of light from the one unblinded window, he reached the Grass-plot. He paused then, leaning against the palisade that surrounded the flag-staff. He heard, rather than saw, the balled flag rustle softly as it hung suspended against the foot of the mast. He would have spat upon it could he have reached it. But he could curse it. To-morrow—nay, this very morning—the ball of bunting would run up quickly to the truck and would reveal itself magnificently as the Union Jack at the precise hour, perhaps, the requisition went in for his coffin. So he cursed it, beneath his breath.

At last he stood within a yard's length of his goal. See that narrow stream of light, shooting outwards from midway up that great rim of massy blackness? It projects from the loophole of the guard-tower at the north-eastern angle of the gaol. Six feet above the loophole stands, as Bill knows well, a soldier, with firelock ever ready; mute himself, save at half-hour intervals when he hurls into the night a grim, ironical 'All's well!' or, more rarely, when he issues a challenge; and his old Brown Bess is mute too—till there is occasion for her to speak. A pace and a half, and Bill would be visible in the flash of light. Thirty-six inches this side of Eternity! And he had always calculated that it would take a drop of ten feet to dislocate his neck. Decidedly death was nearer this way than from the scaffold—by six feet or thereabouts!

Would Reynell do him justice? Would the Ring? Would the Ring, after all, think he was shot by mischance, instead of from his own purpose?

'God!'—again! He had never thought of that! Would his sacrifice be all in vain, then? Suppose that the Ring still held Reynell to his doom? 'God!'

In the agony of doubt he must have exclaimed aloud. Suddenly the challenge parted the darkness.

'Who goes there?'

He did not give himself time for another thought; he stepped boldly into the light.

'Who goes there? Answer, or I fire!'

'Fire, an' be domned t' tha!'

He challenged Fate as well as the soldier. And both answered.

*   *   *

When they bore him into the guard-room he was still alive. He gasped two sentences. 'Yo'll tell—Pe-ake—this be th' doom. An' give my lo-ave t' 'Arry Reynell, 'ull yo?' and in a little while passed out of the ken of an aggrieved System.

Maconochie, bending to view the wound, saw that the ball had entered between the rims of two circles described on the man's chest. One—the larger—was an old scar; the other—the inner circle—was still of a festering newness. The latter was the symbol of Bill's recently gained membership of No. 7 Circle.

'Bony' Anderson,[10] from the signal-station on Mount Pitt, came down to report that there had been no gun-fire from Phillip's at seven o'clock. A boat was despatched, and returned with the body of a suicide. Bill Felix's sacrifice was in vain, after all. Harry Reynell had anticipated the doom.

---

[10] 'Bony' Anderson: the ex-man-o'-war's man whom the System chained on Goat Island, Sydney Harbour, as a warning to his brother-transports, and a source of pleasure to Sydney Sunday excursionists. Maconochie made him a signalman.

IN THE GRANARY

I.

THERE is no doubt that the place was originally devoted to the purpose implied by its name. But history everywhere is prolific of instances in which an institution or thing has been perverted from an originally admirable purpose to a base use.

Captain Piper designed it—Captain Piper, the genial officer of the New South Wales Corps who was so beloved of John Macarthur; afterwards the Naval Officer whose accounts resolutely refused to balance because he had been so obliging as to allow duties payable by his friends to 'stand over' indefinitely; and, later still, the free-handed squire of a Bathurst estate. He was Commandant of Norfolk Island in the years immediately preceding the removal of the Island settlers to their new and poorer homes in Van Demonia. It was his invention.

Eight by six by ten in dimensions; four hundred and eighty cubic feet in capacity. How many bushels of wheat and maize would that contain?

We do not know; all that we can assert is that twenty-two years after Captain Piper had departed from the Island, this eight by six by ten excavated chamber, with the stone floor, and stone walls, and stone ceiling—this windowless room with but one solitary aperture, and that in the roof—was occupied by—what? Stores of maize? Stores of wheat? Bags of ration sugar?

No; nothing so precious. By two convicts.

II.

Piper had designed the chamber to store surplus grain. Again and again had Government barns and store-buildings been broken open by prisoners who insubordinately declined to starve while the stores held stocks of food-stuff, and who preferred a short shrift and a long rope to an empty stomach. And, therefore, Captain Piper resolved to defeat the mutinous and starving rascals. He had this chamber dug out—built in with stone—closed with an iron door in the roof, which door turned upon a pivot and was fastened by padlocked clamps. When he had filled the granary with grain, he favoured it with additional protection by sentries. And, upon the whole, the Captain's plan was successful. Not more than one prisoner died from actual starvation during the period the granary was full of a reserve stock in case the store-ship with supplies from the Old Town failed to make the Island in due course. And he, it is believed, died because he was forgotten. They locked him up in the old gaol cell and quietly overlooked him for ten days. And when they remembered him he had gone to report himself to the authorities of a Higher System.

But that incident is by the way.

Wright was Commandant. And when he took charge he found, in the course of an examination one day, an iron door level with the earth and rusted in its socket of stone. He wondered what it could be for just so long as it took to send a soldier for the blacksmith, and for the time the blacksmith was engaged in forcing the clamps. When the iron plate was made to revolve upon its pin, Captain Wright—a Ghoorka, in after years, let the life out of his body in a vain attempt to find the ex-Commandant's heart—looked down into the cavity, smelt its exhumed mustiness, and, gleefully, smote his thigh with his gloved hand.

'The very thing!' he exclaimed, 'the very thing!'

'Sir?' questioned Overseer Cook, who was in respectful attendance.

'This will do for Freeman and Hansen, Cook. No chance of their getting out of here!'

Not being an officer and gentleman, and not, therefore, wholly intoxicated with the absolutism of power, Overseer Cook shuddered. He was an instance of the square peg in the round hole. Transported for some aimless ranting in a London street over the Peterloo massacre, he was tried under one of the Six Acts, and awarded, in recognition of his patriotism, seven years' residence across the seas. On securing his certificate of freedom, he became a clerk attached to Sydney Police Office, and on the re-settlement of Norfolk Island as a penal establishment, was appointed an overseer. He was at once an exception to one rule and an illustration of another. An ex-convict who became an overseer generally so acted that, between himself and an average 'officer and gentleman' acting as commandant, there was little to choose in respect of brutality. Cook was an exception to this rule. But the rule that a man transported for seditious utterances—for permitting scorching words to pour forth from the volcano of a heart which burnt with a fiery pity for the poor, and a fiery contempt for the social conditions which held the poor in bondage—proved a genial taskmaster to prisoners when clothed with authority, this he illustrated daily. Cook, with every temptation to be otherwise, remained kind-hearted.

He shuddered, and ventured to hint a remonstrance.

'You don't mean, sir, do you, to put those pris'ners here?'

'I do, Cook. What's the use of gaoling them or flogging 'em? No use at all! The scourgers sooner take a flogging themselves than give 'em the lash hearty, and till I build the new gaol, to put 'em into gaol is only to contaminate every man Jack there. I thought of marooning 'em, but I didn't want to lose six or eight lives in getting 'em to the Phillip or Nepean. If any lives were lost in the surf, 'twouldn't be Freeman's or Hansen's. They're both bound to be scragged!'

'But, sir, this vault was never intended for a gaol. According to the talk of the old hands, it must have been a grain-store.'

'Grain-store or not, I'll use it for those ruffians. A brace of staples apiece driven in, and twenty-pound trumpeters,[1] will hold 'em in, or else my name isn't Wright.'

'But, sir—' Cook, maudlinly inclined to take a humane view of things, stumbled in his speech.

'Well, sir?' demanded the Commandant, sharply. 'What objection have you to the course I suggest? We don't want the place for maize, for we have none, and we do want another punishment chamber.'

'Well, Commandant, I was only thinking—'

'Go on, damn it, go on! Don't be all day blurting out your old womanish ideas—I know 'tis something of that sort you have to say. I've heard of you, Cook, before! What the devil Gov'ment meant by sending me bread-and-butter misses who turn sick at a flogging and faint at the use of the tube-gag on the biggest scoundrels unhung, I don't know.'

'Well, sir!' responded Cook, with a new firmness in his voice that told how he resented the insult, 'I was thinking that since that new paper had been started in Sydney 'tis scarcely safe—I say it with all respect—to venture upon unusual punishments.'

Wright's language here became unreportably florid. Who on the Island dared to let the Grub-street hacks know of any of *his* doings, would do so at his peril! And within the limits of his letter of appointment he could punish how and in what way he chose short of mutilation of limb or deprivation of life! And if he had only the press writers there he'd teach 'em to set just authority at defiance and to slander honourable officers— yes, he'd teach 'em, the scurrilous crew of penniless scribblers, who only existed because Gov'ment would not deign to notice their existence!

So, with much garnish of adjectives, spoke the Commandant. And he ended by daring Overseer Cook to communicate a single word of Island intelligence to the journals of the Old Town, and by ordering him to

---

[1] 'Trumpeters.'—Irons which connected the ordinary leg-chains with a bazil riveted around each leg immediately below the knees.

instantly prepare the granary for the reception of those mutinous and conscienceless rascals, Freeman and Hansen.

III.

The Overseer, having no choice, obeyed. When the door or valve of the chamber had been opened some hours, he lowered into it a lighted candle. The flame flickered feebly as the candle touched the floor, but did not go out. The fact eased Cook's conscience somewhat. After all, men could not be suffocated there.

Then carefully, rope-held, he dropped through the aperture and examined the vault. Obviously it had been used as a grain-store. The floor was strewn with maize and wheat-grains. And with equal certainty it had never been appropriated to the purposes of a prison. Cook, as he gasped painfully in the heavy humidity of the atmosphere, reflected that the fact was surprising, for he thought the System was ingeniously eager to introduce into Norfolk Island the most approved methods of the Bastille. And here surely was a chamber that would not have been unfit lodging for the most dangerous State criminal ever honoured by a *lettre de cachet*. The wonder was not that it was now to be used for a prison, but that it had not been so appropriated before.

Eight feet long, six in width, ten feet from the middle of the floor to the edges of the opening in the roof, and nine feet high walls curving slightly to their centre. And when the valve was closed, though outside the magnificent sun shone from the dome of a cloudless sky, darkness palpable and terrifying. Cook cried out to the men above to open the valve; it was but a second before the plate revolved on the pivot; but in that instant the Overseer felt himself blanching. It was a tomb.

He could not hold in his emotion. Withdrawn by the rope, he threw himself upon the ground in an attitude of prayer. 'Christ!' he prayed, 'Christ! let no men be imprisoned there!'

And he sent the smith, who had come up with ring-bolts and chisels, back to his forge. 'Not to-day, George—not, at least, till I have seen the Commandant again.'

The smith returned to his workshop to relate 'Cook's prayer' as a good joke, and the two prisoner-police, who formed the Overseer's personal staff, told of the matter in their enlightened circle, and at dinner at Government House, Captain Wright delighted the surgeon, and the subaltern, and the commissary with his version of the incident.

'And what have you done with the canting cove, Captain?' questioned the Deputy-Assistant-Commissary-General.

'Done! Well, he's packing up by this time, I don't doubt. He's resigned, and returns to the city by the brig next week.'

'Phew!' exclaimed the D.A.C.G. 'That's hot, Wright! Is he going to make a fuss about it?'

'Gad! I don't know nor care. Why should I care what a psalm-singing lag of a constable should say about me? My word will be taken by the authorities, I should hope, before his!' His Honour the Commandant displayed a dignified aspect, and spoke in a confident tone, as though he could safely anticipate in advance an honourable acquittal from any charge that might be preferred against him.

'Yes, but,' delicately hinted the D.A.C.G., ''tis not the Chiefs. 'Tis that wretched *Australian* and *Monitor*. There would be the rub if the fellow took particulars to them.'

'Sir,' replied the Commandant, superbly conscious of his power, 'if Wardell or Hayes or Hall dare impugn my conduct, I'll challenge the first and indict the others for criminal libel.'[2]

'But,' persisted the Commissariat, who was, for sundry reasons connected with contracts, not at all desirous that the light of publicity should beat upon the Gehenna of the waters, 'suppose—er—what—er—they say is true!'

---

[2] He did the last.

'True, sir!' The Captain was nearly forgetting his courtesy as a host, so heated did he become. 'I'd have you know that every action of mine I'm prepared to justify in any court of the Empire. But, pass the wine—we've had more than enough talk about two common pris'ners! Let's forget 'em!'

IV.

It would have been well for those infamous prisoners, Freeman and Hansen, if they had passed utterly from the great man's mind. Unfortunately for them, however, the statement Captain Wright made in evidence before the Supreme Court at a later day, 'that he could not charge his conscience with having overlooked any man on the Island,' was quite true—a thing not to be said of other portions of his testimony. He perfectly remembered them the next morning.

'Reports, sir!' deferentially remarked (with a salute) the gaoler.

'Yes, Thorpe. I'm ready to take them.'

Mr. Thorpe opened his report-book.

'Freeman, sir—foul language and threatening to assault constable who took him his food.'

'Pass Freeman for the present. I propose to deal with him in a new way!'

'Yes, sir. Greene, sir. Found in possession of improper article, sir. Tobacco!'

'I thought he was celled?'

'So he is, sir. No. 5!'

'And ironed?'

'Trumpeters—fifteens—and wall-cuffs.'[3]

---

[3] 'Wall-cuffs.'—Manacles fastening a prisoner's wrist to a wall-staple.

'Then how the devil'—the insulted feelings of the offended System breathed in the Commandant's tones—'did Greene get the tobacco? Some of your men to blame there, Thorpe!'

'No, sir, 'm quite sure o' that. The sentries passed it—' Thorpe paused. He had forgotten that here, with the civil and military command vested in the one person, it was scarcely a wise thing to play the game so familiar to other settlements, of blaming the military for the *lâches* of the 'establishment.'

'Now, Thorpe, be careful. I'll have none of this accusation of the garrison to excuse neglect on your own part or corruption on your men's. Where's the tobacco? Is it produced?'

'No, sir. Th' pris'ner swallowed it, sir! I was goin' rounds after breakfast, and No. 5 stands up and gulps something down, and I knew 'twas tobacco by the smell of his breath.'

'Did you charge him?'

'Of course, sir; but, of course, he denies. He said it was a bit of crust left from breakfast that he was chewing.'

'Oh, a likely story that! You're sure of the smell?'

'Quite, your Honour!' affirmed Thorpe, a tall, fresh-faced ex-soldier, who was not half a bad fellow under Major Anderson, but under Wright was a miniature of that tyrant—he took his cue always from his superiors.

'He is handcuffed to the wall, is he?'

'Yes, sir!'

'One hand only?'

'Yes, sir!'

'Then double my gentleman's irons, and darby the other hand. Next!'

'But, beg parding, sir—what about the bad languidge, sir?'

'Yes, I was forgetting that. Was it very bad?'

'Awful, sir! Made my blood run cold!'

'Four hours' tube-gag! Next!'

V.

The next was a mere non-entity—a 'refusing-to-work' man—the most fervent believer in the Carlylean doctrine of the soul-saving qualities of work would have doubted his creed had he been compelled to work in fifteen-pound trumpeters. He was ordered thirty lashes—*not* on the back. Wright believed punishment on the back was a concession to a morbidity of sentiment.

And the next accused was a nobody too. Said he was ill. Gaoler affirmed he wasn't. Prisoner asked to see doctor. Gaoler said he shouldn't. Prisoner took the Bible, which was the principal—almost the only—furniture of a gaol-cell, and kissed it, swearing he was ill. Gaoler, shocked at the blasphemy, formally charged the man with prevaricating to evade work—threatened to report him—now did so—received Commandant's instructions to reduce the ration of twelve ounces bread and one half-pint of water made by the generous System even to the turbulent spirits in gaol. Gaoler, touching his forehead, pencilled with stubby finger a cabalistic mark against the Nobody's name, and passed to the next offender. Three days hence, he will put the pencil *through* the name. The Nobody has, by that time, done the very best thing he ever did for himself—has taken up permanent quarters in the little cemetery by the sea. The manchineel drops its tears on the nameless mounds of a hundred of such nobodies.

The next accused was Hansen.

'Insubordinate conduct, sir—very insubordinate, sir, I may say.'

'What did he say?'

'Nothing: 'twas not what he said: 'twas what he did!'

'Well, what did he do?'

'Nothing, sir—simply refused to speak!'

'That is his offence?'

'Yes, sir!'

'Pass him for the present. Next!'

But with the next and his successors at that day's court we have nothing here to do. They are to us, as their names appear on the partly-inked, partly-pencilled record before us, mere shadows. 'Dismissed' to one; 'twenty-five' to three; 'one hundred' to a fifth; and a 'spread-eagle' to a sixth: these are the entries against the names of these phantasms. They are only phantasms—let us thank Heaven for that! For surely, could we realise, even at this distance of time, that these names were those of men—shares with ourselves in the glorious possession of life—our hearts would throb and our eyes fill with sympathetic tears at the thought that all of them, save one, passed unheard and untried to punishment.

And Freeman and Hansen—what of them? Up to this date only the prisoners in the gaol had been supplied with 'magpie'—yellow (or brown) and black—clothing, the stock of that parti-coloured finery being too low to admit of its being issued to other than the aristocrats of crime. And therefore when Freeman and Hansen were ordered by the Commandant to be transferred to the granary, they were, as a preliminary to removal, stripped. In lieu of their comparatively warm costume—some idiot of a manufacturer had actually dared to make a batch of magpie stuff of strong half-woollen material instead of cottony shoddy—they were re-dressed, Freeman in the dyed rags[4] of some ex-Hessian soldier, Hansen in Parramatta dungaree. The former's case was not so bad, but the previous tenant of Hansen's suit had been a worker in the wet quarry, whence were obtained the drip-stones so much in demand in Sydney households, and the garments were still soaking when Hansen was compelled to don them. The result was that before they had been twenty-four hours in the granary, Hansen was coughing violently. Disciplinarians like Wright could take little account of consumptive tendencies, and it was reserved for a latter-day Commandant to invent wet-quarry clothing out of condemned blankets, and thus give the quarrymen a working change.

---

[4] 'Dyed Rags.'—A considerable portion of convicts' clothing for many years consisted of army contractors' surplus stock of uniforms made for George the Third's mercenaries.

VI.

The gaol-allowance of food was bread equal to twelve ounces flour, and a half-pint of water daily. The same ration was issued to the tenants of the granary—lucky dogs that they were! The same unstinted allowances and double the space of floor and breathing room as they enjoyed in the goal! Yet—they refused to be happy. That is to say, Freeman. As for Hansen, he did not care after the second day. He was really getting beyond caring for anything.

'Harry,' said Freeman—it was the third night—'I can't stand this!' Hansen was racked with his cough. His solitary thin blanket was no protection against the cold.

'I'm sorry, Bob—but I can't help it, pal. I 'udn't make such a row if t'other hand was free. I'd 'old it in!' He had but one hand free; the other was linked, with a steel clasp, to the wall. The granary was, one should have thought, safe enough for even Freeman and Hansen, without the ingenious accessory of wall-cuffs. But Captain Wright thought otherwise. And to fifteen-pound irons on the men he had added the single-handed steel attachment.

'Stow that stuff, Harry! Cough, if you want to. What I meant was that I can't stand this place for you. Horspital's th' place for you, old chap—an' that—Com'dant'll ha' to put you there or there'll be trouble.'

'Lor, Bob, don't yer take on now, an' get—' The cough interrupted the remonstrance.

'And get what?'

'Into your tantrums on my 'count.'

'Not a bit of it, old chap. 'Tain't on your account at all—leastwise, not altogether. I'm going to break this—tomb business, once and for all! *I* don't mind, Harry—I'm as cosy here as in a cell, or spread-eagled round a lamp-post on a cold night! But it's such chaps as you, old codger—with any amount o' heart, but not a stiver's worth of bodily strength to feed th' blood with. It's for you, and such as you, I'm going to break up this—granary punishment!'

The fellow flung out his words in ascending tones that unmistakably expressed the tense fierceness of passion which was gnawing him. He was liable to be swayed by great gusts of passion, though for weeks together he would be as quiescent as the grave. But the account-keeping gave him no credit for his placid intervals, measuring his nature by its cyclonic periods. And one of those was now upon him—epileptic almost in its violence.

Hansen, who knew his co-prisoner well—they had bolted together, been wound up together[5] on the *Wellington* when on the voyage from Sydney, been flogged, 'cuffed, 'spread-eagled,' celled together—cowered in his own corner, and with his one hand sought to check his coughing, so as not to agitate Freeman the more.

The twilight outside was fading into darkness in the interior, but the sick prisoner saw every movement, every feature of his comrade. Freeman— who was short and sturdy of figure, and who had grievously offended the System, time after time, because, in spite of continued short commons, he would preserve strength, as though his will replenished his sap—knelt down. He knelt sideways to the wall, as the short 'cuff-chain would not permit of his facing it. A suspicious System foresaw that a 'cuffed prisoner might, by thrusting his feet against the wall, secure leverage for the withdrawal of the staple.

Not in prayer did Freeman kneel, but to gain the greater purchase on the steel links which held his right wrist firmly to the wall. And thus kneeling, his broad flanks were drawn in—his upper teeth scored his lower lip to their full depth—his left hand was thrust forward and grasped the 'cuff-chain—the blood shot into his eyes, and left his cheeks so livid that their ghastliness shimmered in the gathering gloom. He hauled once, twice—and then, with a deep groan, an involuntary tribute to

---

[5] 'Wound up together.'—En route from Sydney or V.D.L. to Norfolk Island, prisoners were generally handcuffed to a cable, which passed through the hold and connected with the windlass. On any signs of disturbance, a turn or two of the windlass—and quiet was restored.

overstressed nature, he fell back, his head striking dully the stone floor. For some minutes he lay in the happy enfranchisement of a swoon.

When he recovered, he was comparatively free. Free, that is, to the extent of his 'cuff-shackle. He had pulled out the wall-staple, and the manacle dangled from his wrist.

The effort had been terrible: that last moment of strain, before the stone had yielded up the staple, had clutched his wrist in a constriction as suffocating as the experience of the Laocoon in the coils of the serpent. He could not believe, at first, that it was the staple which had given way: he thought the ring which had grasped his flesh had cut his hand from the arm.

But when he saw what he had achieved, when for the first time for months he realised that he could walk the length of his cell—he had been wall-'cuffed, remember, in gaol also—he sank nervelessly into the corner next Hansen, and, dropping his head on his knees, gasped his relief in tearless sobs. And, so squatting, he passed into slumber. Hansen need not have striven so strenuously to repress his coughing. Freeman's exhaustion conferred upon him the rare boon of a dreamless sleep.

Once only during the night did he seem on the verge of waking. That was when Hansen, who had stinted himself to half his ration of water during the day in order that he might retain some for the thirst of the parching night-hours, dipped into his pannikin the rag which served him as a handkerchief; and then, stretching himself noiselessly towards his sleeping comrade, placed the moistened bit of cotton upon the fevered forehead. Freeman stirred, but did not wake; and perhaps he slept the sounder for the other convict's poor, priceless sacrifice.

VII.

The dawn-light stole into the vault through the aperture in the roof. With a fine generosity Wright had consented to the iron door remaining unclosed, as he concluded the wall-'cuffs held these two dreadful ruffians firmly; so, before Freeman awoke, the sweet, glorious day had sent a shaft of radiance into the darkness. It fell upon Hansen's face and roused him, and he, in turn, gently shook the slumberer.

'Bob!' he said, 'rashins'll be 'ere presently. There's the yard-bell now!'

Freeman turned, and sat up, and recollection coming back as drowsiness vanished, replied, 'Right, Harry, old chap. How's the cough?'

'Not a bit easier, Bob—but hadn't yer better get back to your corner? Rashins'll be 'ere in a jiffy!'

Freeman rose and walked across, and laughed as he crossed the bar of light and held up the dangling steel-clips to glisten in the beam. 'Wouldn't it spoil the Com'dant's breakfast, Harry, to know as I stand here?'

'Is your wrist sore, Bob?'

'Sore ain't a name for it, Harry; but the sea air'll cure it!'

Hansen started in his corner. 'What d'ye mean, Bob? Yer ain't a-thinkin' o' boltin,' are yer?'

Freeman laughed. 'No—no such luck. But I am going for a sea-trip to the Old Town; an' you're going too.'

'What's—what's—the use—of jokin,' Harry?' The question was punctuated with coughs, and vibrated with a poignant despair.

Freeman turned and placed his hand in Hansen's: 'Don't give up, Harry, pal! Don't funk on it! I've sworn to have yer out o' this, an' I will!'

''Ow, Bob, 'ow?'

'I won't tell you, Harry. Ye'll have to trust me. If you don't know, they can't bring you in access'ry!'

And though Hansen tried, he obtained no more satisfaction than that indefinite answer.

*   *   *

Their rations came. 'Catch!' said the 'outer'-billet prisoner who had been detailed by the under-gaoler to deliver the food and drink so magnanimously allowed them. And as he spoke, he bent down and threw the hunks of bread into the corners. And the water he lowered in a pot, with a looped cord—a pint between them. Freeman repeated his previous day's performance, and dragged the can with his feet till he could reach it with his left hand, and divide its contents between the pannikins.

'All right?' questioned the messenger. 'Com'dant 'opes as yer've 'ad a good night!' he continued, with a genial satire in his laugh.

'Hansen oughter see th' croaker,' said Freeman.

'Wot's th' use o' that lay, Bob Freeman? Yer know as Wright's not a bird as'll be caught by that 'ere sort o' chaff. 'Udn't I look a fool now ter report 'Arry 'Ansen sick, an' then by an' by th' doc. comes 'long an' ses he's a-shammin' Abram?' And confident in his own wisdom and the deceit of the two prisoners, he went his way.

'In the last resort the System is often administered by convict understrappers,' wrote Dr. Wardell pseudonymously to his own paper, the *Australian*. 'The great men who rule frequently work through illiterate brutes.'

VIII.

Through the long day that terrible rascal, Freeman, sought to amuse his fellow-*confinée*. With jest and low chant—a loudly-sung song might have procured the tribute of the tube-gag—he sought to help Hansen's spirits to laughter-point. And by one other thing also.

He 'blanketed' his irons. He tore the shoddy stuff into strips, to Hansen's wonderment, and wrapped the pieces round the 'trumpeter' irons, so they should not clank. Then—for Hansen's amusement, so he said—he practised jumping upwards so as to touch the roof with his palms. Not with his finger-tips merely, but with his palms.

Now, his irons were fifteen-pounders. They were light for 'trumpeters.' Still they waxed weightier and weightier as he persisted in his exercise. And if you wish to know the true character of the task which he set himself, try the experiment of jumping with seven-pound dumb-bells fastened to your feet.

Three or four times in quick succession would he leap upwards. Then he would rest and regain breath. And then he would spring up again, until at last he had achieved his end. Thrice running he had touched with both palms open at once the roof within a few inches of the margin of the door-opening. And Hansen, interested, forgot to cough. Like manna to starving people, desert-lost, was his comrade's athletic endeavours to the monotony-damned invalid.

'The night's come soon, Bob,' he said, as the early darkness fell. 'That's 'cos we've had some-think to think about.'

''Tis just that, Harry, pal. An' ye'll see to-morrer'll pass quicker,' Freeman gasped, for he was quite exhausted.

'Wot, agoin' to try it to-morrer again?'

'Rather!' replied Freeman, with a chuckle. And the prospect of further pleasure on the morrow kept him warm in lieu of his blanket.

*   *   *

The yard-bell had swung its ding-dong at the breakfast-hour, and the sound stole over the quarter-mile of vacant ground to the granary. And Hansen urged Freeman, who had been walking up and down the cell, to regain his corner. 'Dick'll be here soon,' he said. To his surprise and alarm, however, Freeman simply smiled, and continued his walk to and fro.

'Bob, are yer crazy? Rashins'll be 'ere, I say.'

'I ain't crazy, Harry, an' I know they'll be here.'

'But he'll cotch yer, Bob!'

'I think the boot'll be on t'other leg, Harry!' answered Freeman.

And it was.

As the steps of the messenger, Dick, were heard approaching, Freeman halted just without the disc of light cast by the aperture upon the stone floor, and so that the bearer of the rations could not see him without peering down.

'Below there, boys!' called Dick. And he repeated the words growlingly as they met with no response.

Then Dick stooped down to peer into the corners.

'Yer lazy wretches—'

He did not live to complete the sentence of reproach. He had spoken thus far when Freeman, under the impulse of the ferocious passion which he had been nursing since the break of the day, sprang mightily upwards. His hands met on the doomed felon's throat, and though Dick was not so maddened by his death agony that he did not strive to force himself backwards, Freeman's grasp did not relax. As the latter was drawn down by his irons, he pulled the semi-conscious Dick after him. A minute later all was over for Messenger Dick.

The felicity of the System was that at every nook and corner of the Regulations and every stage of routine, it provided an opportunity for some one to get hanged. Even the life-saving institution of the granary, you see, had proved the ante-chamber to the gallows.

IX.

For, of course, the System meritoriously hanged Convict Freeman after trial in Sydney; but do what Convict Hansen could by way of impressive appeal to C.J. Sir Francis Forbes to treat him, Hansen, not as a witness but as an accessory before the fact, it declined to hang him.

'Harry Hansen's a-committin' perjury, y' Honour,' said the accused, 'when he says as he suggested the doin' o' Dick. He speaks truth, though, when he says as he was witness. I wanted him to be witness.'

'Why?' shuddered the C.J.

'Because, y'r Honour, I wanted people in the Old Town here to know as a sick lag like Harry there can't get the croaker's 'tendance at Norfolk. I put it to y'r Honour, ain't he sick? an' the Com'dant says he was shammin' Abra'm.'

And the Court looked at the consumptive ruffian, and in its judicial mind gave him a week longer to live than Freeman. And Freeman would 'suffer' on Monday week, and this was Wednesday.

But the Court was wrong.

On the Friday before *his* Monday, Freeman, staring out of one of the dozen fully occupied condemned cells, saw two of the prisoner-wardsmen attached to the gaol-hospital bearing a grey-sheeted form into the corridor. They stopped before his cell. 'Are yer Norfo'k Freeman?' questioned the front bearer.

'Yes! That Harry?'

'This is Hansen. Gov'nor ses as 'ow 'e thort yer'd like ter see th' larst of 'im.' And he turned down the sheet, so that the pinched, peaked features were visible.

'So, Harry,' said the condemned, 'you've got home first, have you? Well, 'tis kind of the 'thorities to let me see you. The fun of it is, though, that they're always so dev'lish kind when 'tis too late.'

As we have no fancy for attempting the impossible, we shall not try and demonstrate that Condemned Convict Freeman was in error in that last remark.

PARSON FORD'S CONFESSIONAL

I.

IT is beyond question that Parson Ford's resolve to keep up the amount of his fee for performing marriages was responsible for the annoyance which visited him on the occasion of our story.

Eight pounds sterling was his fee. Parson Knopwood would do the work for three and take payment in currency; and it was generally the easiest thing for an expert bridegroom to relieve the old man of the money as he was returning home the same evening. When Parson Bob performed the ceremony, he invariably celebrated the event at the 'Hole in the Wall,' the favourite public-house, where his welcome was always warm and his chalk-score deep, and he would seldom proceed homewards to Cottage Green till the everlasting stars came out in their glory and flaunted their drunkenness in his shame-stricken eyes. At least that was what the cheery old chaplain used to say as he stumbled over Macquarie-street cobble-stones. 'Wheresh O-rion? Shure I saw O-rion (*hic*) jush now!—'sh gone! Shtrange—th' bleshed (*hic*) stars dansh about so. Tell Gov-en-or!' And then perhaps the bridegroom, who had paid him about eleven o'clock that morning £3 in paper notes or dollars, would take his arm respectfully to help the reverend gentleman along—and himself to the £3. Sometimes, indeed, the bridegroom would not wait to tender his assistance. This was when the fee had been paid in forged notes, as several times happened.

Now, Parson Ford was a steady, pure, and sober man, and was not in the least inclined, when he became Principal Chaplain on Bobby Knopwood's official retirement, to view with aught but displeasure the irregularities

99

which his predecessor had tolerated. He never got drunk; he knew the difference between forged currency notes and general currency by the 'feel'—he could tell by the touch, so he said, any one tradesman's notes from every other man's—and he went home by dusk, or if detained after dark by pastoral duty, only after he had emptied the contents of his pockets and his fob into the keeping of a trusty acquaintance or officer of the garrison. Consequently, being possessed of these defects, he was not at this time beloved by the lower, or, indeed, any orders of society. Not till later did even the official classes come to believe in him. A community in which the heads liked to be drunk by mid-day, where matrimonial arrangements seldom were entered into except for the purpose of securing an additional grant of land or a right to other property, and where it was unsafe for a person to be out of doors after nightfall, because of his liability to be robbed, if not by unofficial criminals, by the men of the watch, was not prepared to take to its bosom at once a strong-minded cleric, whose pockets were never worth robbing, who would not drink to excess, whose only vice was snuffing, and who was so much of a Puritan that he had even admonished his Honour the Lieutenant-Governor for having a plurality of paramours. And when Parson Ford was so ill-advised as to raise the marriage-fee to eight pounds sterling, he placed the coping-stone to the edifice of his unpopular life. One and all, high and low, Lieutenant-Governor and lumberyard transport, who would not have married his 'jomar' if the marriage-fee had been nothing, indignantly resented the step.

Why people who disdained marriage should have been thus irritated we do not positively know. We can only suppose it was by reason of that perverse trait of humanity which prompts it to value the thing which is beyond reach. If only a few couples could get married, nearly everybody would either wish to go through the ceremony or affect the desire to do so. Perhaps some such consideration had influenced Parson Ford in raising his fee. He assessed matrimony at a pecuniary value far beyond the reach of the mass of persons, and instantly they began to denounce the avarice and the injustice and the wickedness which prevented them from obtaining the blessing of the Church on their very irregular alliances. They forgot they had not rushed to the altar when the terms were only three pounds.

II.

'I hear, Mr. Ford,' remarked his Honour, as the parson paid him the usual morning visit exacted from all Hobart Town gentlemen who drew pay from the Colonial chest, 'that you have caused it to be known that your marriage-fee is to be eight pounds in future?'

'That is my fixture, your Honour,' replied the chaplain.

'But I do not know whether I can allow it! You know that the Governor in Sydney has fixed the fee at four pounds?'

'Guineas, your Honour,' gently corrected the parson. 'But that is within two described parishes. I am sure of my legal rights on the matter.'

'But the moral effect, Mr. Chaplain—the effect! Have you sufficiently thought of that? A heavy fee is—ahem—an impediment to marriage!'

One great virtue had Parson Ford. He looked over a lot of things in persons of authority, but, when put on his mettle he never winced before a Governor, whether he was only a 'Lieutenant,' or whether he was the omnipotent 'General.' He faced his Honour now, and said distinctly, with an uncourtier-like acidity of tone: 'Would it have proved so in *your* case, your Honour? If so, I'll reduce it!'

And his Honour took the unpleasant thrust pleasantly. His wine-reddened face was not unusually flushed as he responded: 'Well, well, if you must have it so, you must, I s'pose, Mr. Ford. But don't you think you can make it currency, instead of sterling?'[1]

'With all respect, sir, I do not think I can. My object is to make the ceremony valued in the eyes of the people, and I conceive there is no

---

[1] 'Currency' and 'Sterling.'—The difference in value in Davey's time varied from 121/2 to 25 per cent.

better way of doing it than to attach an expense to its performance. You have seen, your Honour, that Mr. Knopwood's low charges did not encourage marriages. Now, we will see what *my* method will do.'

'Very well, Mr. Ford, very well, have your own way. I think you are mistaken, but it's your lookout, and not mine. I'm not—h'm—my brother's keeper—of his morals, at all events. That's your duty.'

And with this, his Honour bowed his reverence out, helped himself to a glass of Spanish wine from a bottle which, one of a dozen, had been presented to him by his former comrade-in-arms, John Macarthur, in Sydney—Capt'n John had bought it at a sale of certain prize booty in the year '5, and treasured it greatly—and set to work to devise a scheme by which to revenge himself upon the clergyman. Davey was not given to vindictiveness, but he dearly liked a jest, and when by the same stroke he could have both his joke and his revenge, he would have fallen below the level of his drunken, rollicking, immoral old self if he had refrained from applying it. He had all the qualities of a good Governor except dignity, firmness, purity, honour, sobriety, and magnanimity.

As the result of his reflections he outlined a plan which, in the bosom of his irregularly constituted family circle at Government House, was fairly elaborated that same night. It was necessary, you see, for him to use an intermediary in the business. He rather prided himself on his free-and-easy manners. Had he not made his *début* in the colony in his shirt-sleeves, excusing himself on the score of its being too—hot to wear full regimentals? Had he not established the custom of drinking and smoking in court? Was it not he who had stopped the trial-gang on their way to the wharf, and treated each of the unfortunates to a drink of rum-punch and a churchwarden pipe at Half-Hanged Jack's beershop? Did he not accept kindly their thankful 'God bless yer Honour!' and wish them in return a fair trial, and, if God and the Judge pleased, an easy death? And was it not, too, his identical old blackguard self who, instead of enclosing to Sydney with the depositions of evidence against a convicted forger, the forged note for *threepence*, put the note, and therefore the evidence, into the fire, with the remark that a throat that could give out 'Tom Bowling' so well, was too good to be fitted with a throat necklace? As a matter of fact, 'free and easy' was an absurdly weak term to apply to Lieutenant-Governor Davey's relaxed manners. Nevertheless, he felt it was 'not quite the cheese'—the phrase is not ours but the Governor's—for him to place himself in direct communication with the principal in the plot he had contrived for the discomfiture of Parson Ford. 'No, Julia,' he said to the presiding madam of the week—his two 'ladies' took week about in doing the honours of his private table (his legal family living quite apart)—'it won't be quite the cheese, my duck, for me to see the little dears at the Factory. One of you will have to do that for me.'

'Oh,' simpered madam—she was the identical pretty piece of frailty respecting whom Captain Colnett, of H.M.S. *Glatton*, had quarrelled with Governor King,[2] and the twelve years since the row had only matured her charms—'anythin' to please yer, dear Gov'nor—an' really, ye know, none of us leddies like Parson Sniff an' Snuff! Bobby's my 'dea of a parson. Ain't he yours, dear Gov'nor?'

'I'm with ye, madam, in everything, as ye know,' replied the Governor— whose gallant speeches were not yet intermingled with hiccoughs. 'Ah, old Bobby never interfered between me an' ye, did he, dear? But ye'll attend to the Factory, Ju, without fail before Monday evening? Ye know, 'twould never do for his Honour, the Gov., to be known in the business.'

'Oh, lud, your Honour, how squeamish we're gettin' all at once,' tittered the sorceress of the week; 'why, ye'll be turnin' saint yourself soon an' 'll cry 'Fie!' an' blush when I do this.'

And, bending forward, she pressed with her ruby lips the viceregal forehead. Madame Julia knew the ways of Government in early Van

---

[2] Considering that, as a rule, Rusden, the historian, damns the cause he advocates, it is an unfortunate thing for Governor King's fame that Rusden defends his conduct in the Colnett case. King's action appears, however, eminently creditable to him, even in the light of the superior morality of this generation. Tested by contemporary canons, it reflected infinite honour upon him.

Demonian days. Also which side her bread was buttered. She was better off with Colonel Davey than with Captain Colnett, R.N. Immeasurably.[3]

III.

What the official lights-o'-love achieved the sequel will show. The Governor did, however, make a specific contribution to the plot, but he kept the knowledge of it from his Cleopatras. He chuckled mightily as he added his fragment of fuel to the flame which was to scorch Parson Ford. He penned the following—

Private.

Government House, THURSDAY.

REVEREND SIR,—The words that passed between us on a delicate subject have afected me, and have not failed to impres me. As one means of helping to releeve me from his reverence's sensure it is likely that a warm discourse on the subject by which you will understand I mean the iregular connections which your reverence does not approve of, on Sunday coming, would strengthen my hands, for I have come to the conclusion that my honourable position does demand from me conduct which would not remain open to your Reverence's objection.

Your Reverence's obedient servant,

(Sd.) THOMAS DAVEY, Lieutt.-Gov.

To the REVEREND THEOPHILUS FORD,
at St. Davids Parsonage.

Like the illustrious Wellington, Colonel Davey was weak in orthography and in grammar, but the Rev. Mr. Ford was too well acquainted with official eccentricities of the kind to dwell upon those features of the document. What impressed him was the possibility it held out of a reform in popular morals. And he resolved to accept the hint, 'and to give it 'em warm.'

---

[3] She boxed Colnett's ears. He retaliated.

It was on the succeeding Sunday that he rose to the occasion. It was the first Sunday in the month, consequently a muster-Sunday, and pretty well everybody in Hobart Town was crowded into the church or within its precincts. A muster-Sunday for the bond or ticket-of-leave classes was, of course, compulsory, and those who were emancipated or 'free' by 'servitude' were almost as regular in attendance, for, besides the fun of the thing, there was the gratification of witnessing the subjection of others to a procedure once so galling to themselves. Then the few people who 'came free' and the 'garrison ladies' came also to witness the spectacle. It was *so* amusing, you will understand, to note the distress of some poor 'ticket-of-leave,' as, from some more or less real peccadillo, his 'ticket' was withdrawn, perhaps a little home or business sacrificed, and he himself re-consigned to the purgatory of the lumberyard or the hell of the road-gang. In an epoch when popular entertainments were rare, the Sunday muster was highly valued by all except those who were compelled to attend it.

On this Sunday the muster was before Church. The Muster-Master, as though in anticipation of the coming storm, was righteously indignant in the cases of a couple of dissolute fellows, who, having permission to marry, had gone no nearer the altar than the broomstick. They pleaded Parson Ford's increased fee, but 'twas no use. Their tickets were withdrawn, and they were ordered to present themselves before the Police Magistrate in the morning for sentence.

This incident had so agreeably entertained the 'free' people, 'irregularly-attached' or not, that they would have been prepared to enjoy even a less thrilling sermon than that Mr. Ford preached to them. Therefore, when he gave out his text from Ecclesiastes vii. and 26th—

> And I find more bitter than death the woman whose heart is snares and nets, and her hands as bonds; whoso pleaseth God shall escape from her; but the sinner shall be taken by her—

they settled down with an unusual zest. They knew by instinct something interesting was coming.

Illustrating his theme by pretty well every Scriptural passage having the remotest relation to it, the preacher denounced the iniquity of 'irregular connections.' Then, by way of contrast, he painted the virtues of the typical British home, drew tears from many eyes by a description of the conjugal felicity which prevailed in the palace of the Sovereign—he was discreetly silent as to the Regent—and, having insinuated a refined advertisement of his reasons for raising the marriage-fee—'that which costs nothing or next to nothing,' he said, 'is never valued,'—he concluded with a most touching peroration. With eyes alternately directed to the roof and upon the viceregal pew, he thanked Heaven that he had it from the best, he might say the *very best*, authority that *henceforth* the Local Representative of that pure and pious Personage whose virtues added lustre to the Crown of England, contemplated reflecting *in his person and establishment* the example of his Gracious Sovereign. With so striking an exemplar on the spot, he reminded his hearers that there would be no excuse for their permitting their irregular unions to remain unblessed by the Church and unsanctioned by the Law.

The effect was tremendous. New South Wales and Van Demonia in the early days had, of course, no opportunity of showing how a C—— could throw an aristocratic splendour over the gallows, or how a H—— could transform by grace of manner a niggardliness of expenditure into a refined economy; but yet they possessed, all things considered, as devoted a regard for the representative of the throne as we can claim to-day. The eye of the congregation seemed fixed upon the broad shoulders of the Lieutenant-Governor as he sat a few yards away from the pulpit. A kindly shadow from a pillar prevented, however, all save those in the immediate vicinity observing that the viceregal form shook as though with suppressed emotion. Frequent applications of a yellow handkerchief to his eyes further testified to the impression the sermon had made upon him. Was the Colonel really going to reform? Was he smitten with sorrow for the past, and moved by passionate desire for better things in the future? It seemed so, indeed, and one portly merchant—a conditional pardon man from Sydney-side—reflected ruefully that, eight pounds or no eight pounds, he'd be obliged to follow the Governor's example, if the great man really meant to abandon his harem.

But the merchant and those who noticed his Honour's emotion need not have been afraid. True, he did wipe tears from his eyes, but—it pains us to say it—they were of mirth. The Colonel of Marines was all the time wondering to himself how Jess and Ju were taking the sermon. He had never gone so far as to install them in the viceregal pew—the ladies of his family proper would have drawn the line at that—but he knew they were in church. He'd have given a day's pay in sterling money, and not in those rascally rupees which were worth no more than eighty per cent of their nominal value, to have been able to look round and wink at the sweet creatures. But that he dare not do: it would have spoilt the sport, for did he catch their eyes in return he would to a certainty burst into laughter. Accordingly, he had to wait till afternoon.

IV.

The Parson dined with his Excellency, and received the latter's great compliments for the unstinted and fervid morality of the discourse. The Colonel now coincided with Mr. Ford as to the wisdom of the increased fee, and expressed a hope that not many months would elapse before it would be—er—as difficult to find an irregularly-attached couple in Hobart Town as a needle in the proverbial truss of hay! And the joy which is generated by the consciousness that a good work is meeting with the applause of the high and mighty settled upon Parson Ford's soul as he bade his Honour good-bye, and betook himself to the church for afternoon service. It was a joy undimmed by the least doubt as to the sincerity of the Governor's conversion.

After second service he was asked to tea at the table of one of the two married ladies of the garrison. The garrison was, matrimonially considered, very badly organised indeed. With the exception of two, the ladies who looked after the comfort of the officers, drawing married men's lodging and fuel allowances, however frequently they quarrelled among themselves, had one characteristic in common. They possessed no certificate of marriage—at least, they owned no certificates that sanctified their present relationships. And now, in consequence of Parson Ford's sermon, the virtuous and duly married two were more determined than ever to look down upon their unlicensed sisters of the quarters. Accordingly, as a preliminary, they mutually arranged an applausive tribute to that dear man, the clergyman, who at last had put his foot resolutely down 'on the shocking, *the really too shocking*, state of things that prevailed in the town, and particularly within our *brother officers'* quarters, you know, dear.' Mrs. Lieutenant Bobbin had wished to do the honours, and invited Mrs. Captain D'Ewes, her sister in matrimonial distinction, to take tea with her and the dear parson, but Mrs. Captain D'Ewes, by virtue of her husband's rank, pressed for the privilege of first entertainment, which Mrs. Bobbin at once effusively and affectionately conceded. And so at half-past five o'clock the Rev. Theophilus found himself seated at a table with Mrs. D'Ewes and Captain D'Ewes, and Mrs. Bobbin and her Lieutenant. It may be remarked, by the way, that the Lieutenant's experience of wedded life was rather regarded in the town as strong evidence of the advantages of single blessedness.

Mr. Ford having said grace (the circumstance from its unusual nature deserves to be chronicled), and accepted some of the hospitalities of the table, his hostess lost no time in expressing her congratulations on his proper, very proper, course that day. And did he really think his Honour would alter the disgraceful, very disgraceful, condition of Government House society?

'I am, ma'am, firmly convinced in my own mind he really contemplates a change of conduct,' affirmed the Parson.

'Then—then—those women—Oh, really, Mr. Ford, I blush for my sex to think such things are possible! And will his Honour *at once* dismiss them to the Factory?' Thus spoke the virtuous Bobbin dame.

'I am quite of opinion that he will do so. In fact, I may tell you—in confidence, ladies, of course—that I believe they have already been returned there!'

'No!' exclaimed both ladies in a breath.

'Indeed, I think so. As I was taking off my surplice in the vestry, the matron of the Factory came in and said that the Governor's ladies—you know, ma'am, that the way those low-class women *will* speak of these disgraces to their sex—'

'Yes, indeed!' indignantly said Mrs. D'Ewes, 'this misuse of words ought to be put down! And the matron said?'

'That those sinful women had been driven out to the Factory. The matron, bringing in the rest of the Protestant women for afternoon service as usual, met them half-way. They looked in a fine fluster—to use Mrs. Chubb's words—just as though the consequences of their sin had at last fallen upon them.'

'Ah!' said Mrs. D'Ewes, 'there comes an end to all wrong-doing sooner or later.'

'Why,' said the Lieutenant, 'didn't the matron stop and ask them why they were going out?'

'Oh, Lieutenant, you don't know what a trouble 'tis to that poor woman to get those drabs of Factory girls to church!—she could not attend to anything else! She has to bring them in two batches—morning and afternoon—for it would take her whole staff to march the lot in together, and she must, of course, leave two or three wards-women behind to look after the sick ones.'

'We'd always tell off a corporal's guard to help her,' said Captain D'Ewes, flippantly. 'Our men would not object to guard-duty there. "Guardians of beauty, if not of virtue," and so on, eh, Bobbin?'

Bobbin, with his spouse's eye upon him, dare not acquiesce verbally, but in his heart he approved of his comrade's sentiment. Of course, their respective wives were not aware that among the Lotharios of the camp, D'Ewes and Bobbin were included, even though they were married. Had he wished to reply, however, he would not have found it possible to do so, for Mrs. D'Ewes sharply remonstrated with her husband.

'I think, Captain,' she said, 'that you should keep your wit for the low associates of the barrack-room. Remember, a clergyman is present, if you have no respect for ladies. And now, dear Mr. Ford, I *should* like so much to know whether those—those creatures are really at the Factory! You, I suppose, will find out in due course?'

'Oh, to-morrow, ma'am, is my usual Factory day—Monday succeeding Muster-Sunday, y' know!'

'Oh, yes,' broke in that ribald D'Ewes, 'tomorrow's your confessional day, is it, Mr. Ford?'

'My what—sir?' returned the astonished Parson, who was nothing, if he was not a sturdy Evangelical.

'That, I believe, sir, is the term given in the town to your—ah—method of interrogating those frisky young madams at the Factory, of whom you're so fond.'

'Sir!' exclaimed the insulted Parson, rising.

'D'Ewes!' appealed his better-half.

'Captain D'Ewes!' ejaculated the horrified Mrs. Bobbin, whose husband simply chuckled to himself under cover of the storm.

And though D'Ewes apologised, and handsomely withdrew the imputation, which, he averred, was merely a jocular nothing, the Parson's sense of injury was not appeased until both Mrs. D'Ewes and Mrs. Bobbin had consented to accompany him to the Factory on the morrow. 'Then, ladies, I beg you'll interrogate every woman for yourselves. Ask them what questions you like as to my treatment of them, and see if I've ever acted in a manner unbefitting my sacred office!'

As a simple fact, Parson Ford could not have played more nicely into his adversaries' hands than when he extended that invitation. Davey's plan had been merely to suggest a very naughty idea to the frail fair ones in Mrs. Chubb's charge, and to trust to chance for the result finding its way to the knowledge of the townspeople. But here Ford himself had provided the means for his own discomfiture.

V.

On the Monday afternoon, the Rev. Theophilus, accompanied by Mesdames D'Ewes and Bobbin, was respectfully welcomed by Mrs. Chubb. As the matron made her final curtsey, she said—

'Twelve new ones, your Rev'runce!'

'All—ahem—er—delicate?'

Mrs. Chubb simpered and looked down. 'Yes, sir!' she said.

'Now, ladies,' and Mr. Ford turned to the garrison ladies, 'of course you don't understand what Mrs. Chubb means?'

'No—not exactly, Mr. Ford,' said Mrs. D'Ewes.

'Well, I must tell you, ma'am. You know, of course, why so many girls are sent back to the Factory from service?'

Mrs. Bobbin blushed. Mrs. D'Ewes didn't, but replied 'Yes.'

'Well, in the interests, first of morality, and then of the finances of the colony, I'm determined to put a stop to that sort of thing, ladies!'

'Quite right, I'm sure,' said Mrs. D'Ewes.

'Quite right, sir,' echoed Mrs. Bobbin.

'Now, there's only one way, and that is to punish the fathers of the children. But to reach the fathers you must know their names.'

'Of course, Mr. Ford!' said both ladies together.

'That is why, then, I have what the Captain very improperly called my confessional, Mrs. D'Ewes. I interrogate each girl separately as to the paternity of her child. Now, to-day, I will ask you ladies to pursue my inquiries for me. Have you any objection, ladies? Then you can tell the Captain the nature of my method.'

'No objection at all,' chorused the gentle beings.

'Then, as there are twelve to be examined, may I suggest you take six, Mrs. D'Ewes, and you the other six, Mrs. Bobbin, and I'll simply look on!'

The twelve girls—they were nearly all on the youthful side of womanhood—were ranged in a row, each standing by the foot of her pallet. Some were quivering with suppressed shame—or laughter. Others were biting their lips. But all were silent till the interrogation began.

Humming a hymn, Parson Ford walked up and down. His back was to the line of women, and consequently he did not see the startled looks which were bestowed upon him and then upon each other by the two ladies. By the time, however, he turned in his walk, each interrogator had examined her second girl, and as she obtained a reply, she glanced so strangely at the clergyman that he could not help but notice her manner. He put the singularity of the look down, however, to some surprising revelation. 'Revelations' under the like circumstances were so common, that they had long since ceased to be surprising to him.

As Mrs. Bobbin interrogated her third girl, Mrs. D'Ewes finished the examination of her fourth. They exchanged a look of horror—then moving simultaneously into the centre of the room, they exclaimed together—

'Oh, Mr. Ford! You wretch!' called Mrs. D'Ewes.

'Mr. Ford, you're a hypocritical villain!' cried Mrs. Bobbin, and she hysterically searched for her handkerchief.

'Ladies!' exclaimed Parson Ford, not believing his ears.

'Yes, sir, I'm glad I came to-day to unmask a scoundrel! Each of these four girls says *you* are the father of her child!' cried Mrs. D'Ewes.

'Madam!'

'And—oh—infamous!—these three girls all say—they—owe—their—ruin to you!' gasped Mrs. Bobbin, in tears.

'And I say the same!' said a girl as yet uninterrogated.

'He's the father of my child too!' said another.

'And of ours!' cried the rest in chorus.

Under this terrible avalanche of accusation Parson Ford was dumb!

*   *   *

Governor Davey and his 'leddies' had calculated only on surprising Parson Ford himself—by bribing the girls with a ticket-of-leave apiece to allege that he, the clergyman, was responsible for her presence in the lying-in ward of the Factory. They had not contemplated so astonishing a success for their little plot, as was achieved through Ford's invitation to the garrison ladies.

Not for many years was Ford allowed to forget this episode. Governor Arthur, fifteen years afterwards, referred, at a birthday dinner, to Parson Ford as one of the 'fathers of the colony,' and was immensely surprised at the uproarious laughter his compliment elicited from all colonists present—save Ford.

THE HEART-BREAKING OF ANSTEY'S BESS

I.

IF ever there was a woman who had a splendid chance of settling herself in life, it was Anstey's Bess—otherwise Elizabeth Sandy, No. 24–175, per *Arab* (1). Not to say anything at all of the proposals of lesser men—not even dwelling particularly on the honour done her by Jorgen Jorgenson, former Governor of Iceland and present magistrate's clerk at the neighbouring township of Oatlands, who would have wedded her without (so he informed her) 'a paper thruppenny'[1] of dower—when Mr. Thomas Anstey's free overseer, Franky Manning, laid his honest heart and his hundred-acre grant, with all appurtenances thereon, at her feet, she was tendered an exceptionally fine opportunity of making a match. Nevertheless she refused.

'I am quite comfortable here, thank'ee, Mr. Manning,' she said, 'an' the master and mistress are kind, an' I'm desperate fond of the childer. An' I'm as happy as I want.'

'But you can be as happy as all this and be your own mistress too, Bess,' pleaded the stalwart Manning. 'Won't ye think better of it? I'll treat ye kind!'

---

[1] 'Paper thruppeny.'—Tradesman's promissory-note of the value of threepence: negotiable only by persons other than the maker at one penny.

'I don't doubt that, Mr. Manning, an' I don't say as it's not a fine chance, but—it's no use. I've made up my mind to stay here till I die, or—' She paused, as though she had already said too much.

'Or what, Bess?'

'Never mind!'

'Till ye get your freedom!'

'Yes, yes—my freedom!' But the exclamation was hurried and confused. As well it might be, for the explanation was not true.

'But the master says as ye'll not apply for your ticket, Bess, and ye won't get a ticket, much less a pardon, without asking for it. Are ye too happy here to ask for freedom?'

'That's it, that's it.'

'No, Bess, there's something else, I'm sure. You're not so happy but that freedom won't make ye happier, specially if ye get with freedom a home of your own.'

'No, no! It's no use, Mr. Manning. Besides, why, you ought to marry a free woman, not me—a lag.'

'D—— the lag—saving your presence, Bess! And even supposing Mr. Anstey couldn't get your pardon just for the asking for it, my love—the love of a square man, though p'r'aps I say it as shouldn't, Bess—will clear your record as though ye'd never been sent out.'

'Ah, that's good of you to say it, Mr. Frank; but you wouldn't like your—your childer to be pointed out for a lag mother's childer.'

Her wooer brought his great hand to his thigh with a resounding clap.

'Who'd dare to raise a word against *my* wife? I'm a free man I'm rich now as men go—I'll be richer by and by. No, none dare say that against your children if they were mine too, Bess! Don't be afraid of that, my dear! Come, Bess, say ye'll have me, and I'll beg Mr. Anstey to ask for your pardon at once. He'll get it, sure. I've been a good servant to him, and so have you, Bess. Now, say yes!—there's a good girl!'

The woman, still comely and fresh-featured for all her thirty-six years, with thick coils of reddish-brown hair, deep-arching eyebrows and milk-white teeth, showing the self-respect so seldom retained by the 'assigned female,' bent her face into her hands. The appeal stirred her, and her whole being quivered with the struggle between the craving to say 'yes' and the knowledge she ought to say 'no.' The ration print-dress of the convict-woman did not always cover the sensibilities of the drab, though Governor Arthur thought so.

Manning waited. He would not further harass her by so much as a glance, so while she pondered he gave a glance to the field adjacent to that in which they were standing. Something there attracted his attention. The ploughing-'teams' were stationary, and instead of the creaking and jingling of the gear, he heard angry voices in excited threats. One voice sounded above the rest, and as he distinguished it, he turned sharply to her.

'Bess, I can't wait any longer, now—though there's still time to say "yes," dear. The men are rowing again—wherever that young scoundrel Davies is there's bound to be trouble if I am not by. I'll come again to-night, Bess—unless'—he paused to grasp the hands which were now clasped on her bosom—'unless it's "yes" *now*, Bess?'

It might have been into ears of stone that he poured his words. Her hearing was intent for another voice than his—that much he understood, for there was straining in her eyes and in her attitude, and the colour came and went in quick rushes to and from her cheeks.

'Bess, Bess, what is the matter? What is it? Are you ill?'

'No—yes! Oh, go away, Mr. Manning—an' don't talk to me of love while that—while that's there!' She threw out her hands as though to push him away.

'What d'ye mean? While what's there?'

'Go, oh, go! Don't you see he—they are fighting! Go, do go—or mischief'll be done, Mr. Manning!'

It was quite time for him to go. From the adjoining paddock came cries of his name, mingled with bitter imprecations, and the group of convicts reeled stormily. He rushed towards the fence which separated the paddocks, and, as he clambered over, looked back.

The woman was prostrate on the sward. He could see the convulsive movements of her hands as they clutched at the grass-tufts.

II.

He could not go back to her, though he troubled greatly, in his simple, strong fashion, that he could not. The fight was proceeding, for the combatants were so enraged that they did not see his coming, and unless he interposed literally with his whip of authority, the contest might end in the infliction of serious injury, if not in murder.

'Stop, there—stop, Davies—New!' He cut at the combatants with his lash of rawhide, and struck them into silence and a sullen inactivity.

The ploughs at work were two, and, meeting on parallel furrows, a dispute had occurred between a man of each team. To each plough were harnessed eight convicts of various ages and statures. Beside Anstey, of Anstey-Barton, only one settler—Bisdee—flagrantly defied the System's economy by indulging in such weak extravagance as to put eight men to a plough. Most land-tillers holding assigned labour displayed a judicious regard for the methods most in favour with the authorities, and employed no more than four. And the Ansteys and the Bisdees were equally opposed to the System in another respect—each discountenanced the sharp pointed goad so generally used by the other settlers. The solitary instrument of persuasion permitted by either gentleman was the strip of untanned hide, and this solely on the ground that its use was necessary to prevent the shirkers throwing the strain of the draught on the willing workers.

'What's this all about?' demanded Manning. 'You, Davies, again! Have you forgotten that I said I'd have you up before Mr. Anstey if you quarrelled again this week?'

Neither of the offenders answered, but Davies, in response to the special inquiry from himself, shrugged his shoulders contemptuously. He was a youth apparently in his eighteenth or nineteenth year, and, save for the scowl, evidently habitual, on his face, would have been handsome.

'Answer, I say!' repeated the overseer.

'Well, if you must know, that—cur, New, there, lied. That's all. And'—a studied impertinence was in his tone as he continued—'as I'm not an officer of the field police, or a free man, I didn't believe in lying, and I hit him!'

'That tongue of yours will get you into serious mischief yet, Davies, if you don't take care. But that's no answer to my question. What did New say?'

'Ask New himself—I decline to repeat a lie even at second hand. But—'

'But what?'

'I warn him that if he dare say to you, in my hearing, even now, what he said before, I'll strike him again, even if you flog me the next moment!'

'This is rank insubordination, and even Mr. Anstey himself wouldn't pass it over. New, tell me what you said. You needn't care for the lad's threats.'

'Care! The fellow—a wizened-featured, stunted Londoner. Wot should I care for 'im? H'im as good as 'im hany day. An' this his wot hi ses, sir—'

'New!' The boy, Davies, threw into the word at once both a challenge and a warning.

'New!' mimicked the other. 'That for you!' He made a vulgar gesture as he spoke. 'This his wot hi ses, Mr. Mannin'—I axed 'im 'ow many kisses 'e give to that 'ere Bess for all th' grub she brings 'im. An' then 'e 'its me, an' hi 'its back!'

'What Bess—what woman?' cried Manning. Rude and uncultivated as he was, he shrank from the possibility that the name which fell so lightly from the wretch's lips was that of the woman to whom he had given his love.

'Vy, Bess that's hup to the 'omestead—Anstey's Bess, o' course!'

Each 'team' was harnessed in pairs by swingle-trees. Davies, the 'off-leader' of one, while New was speaking, and while Manning and the cluster of convicts were intent upon that fellow's words, had stooped and unhooked the swivels which held his own chains to the bar. A length of nearly three feet of inch-links was thus loose in his hand, save that one end was attached to the leathern bazil which encircled his waist. Before New could complete his jibe at the expense of Anstey's Bess, the lad had swung the unattached iron into the telltale's face.

Manning, momentarily staggered by the association of Bess's name with this wastrel of the convict-gang, was recalled to himself by the assault. Although Davies had gathered the length of chain once more in his hands as if to wield it again as a weapon, Manning rushed on him, and, dropping his own whip, seized the youth's wrists.

'I've put up with your conduct long enough, Davies,' he exclaimed, 'but this is going too far. Mr. Anstey shall know of this.'

The boy made one ineffectual attempt to free himself from that mighty grasp, and then, owning the mastery, but still defiant, looked the overseer full in the face, and exclaimed: 'A fig for Anstey! A fig for you! A fig for anybody and everybody in this cursed country—a country of lags who ought to be free men and of free men with the spirit of lags.' Then, as Manning, still holding the lad's wrists, called to take the handcuffs from his, the overseer's pocket, he went on: 'Oh, damn you, Manning—I'll get even with you for this! I've sworn on the lag's Bible[2] I'll do for any man who forces the darbies on me!'

The bracelets snapped on the wrists through which the blue veins were still visible beneath the sunburnt tan.

---

[2] The Newgate Calendar was so called. A transport would go to great straits to procure a copy of this notorious book, or, if it were once in his possession, before he would part with it.

III.

The teams—one man short in each—resumed their ploughing. Tragedies might be enacted, hearts might break in the process, but Anstey's grants had to be prepared for the spring sowing and the autumn harvest. Up and down, one working to the east side of the paddock, the other to the west, scoring with the same furrows the chocolate earth and their own hearts. No task so tore the natures of convicts as that of hauling the plough. Much of their work seared, but the flesh closed over the cicatrices; but the ploughshare cut a wound that rankled for ever, because the work was beasts' work. Yet Anstey's plough-'teams' should have been happy in knowing that, though their work was that of the lower animals, their food was still that of the man. Anstey was unlike C——, who sleeps in Melbourne cemetery in sure and certain dread of a terrible resurrection, and under twelve hundred pounds' worth of lying marble. C——, moved by a sense of the appropriate, fed his plough-cattle on oatmeal and water. 'The fodder of beasts for beasts' work' was his maxim—and his grand-daughter will be presented at Court this year.

For two days the 'teams' worked each a man short. Then the proper allowance of draught was renewed. The number of eight was restored: Davies and New came back. They had been into Oatlands. Davies was reticent with his fellow-cattle. But New was discursive enough for both.

''E was impident to the beak, an' jawed the hoverseer, an' 'e ses that 'e 'ud risk Jack Ketch to 'av 'is go for Mannin.' An' Mannin,' he only larfs, an' begs the beak to let 'im orf easy for a-strikin' me, an' 'e never ses no word at all about cheekin' 'im, so the beak lets 'im orf with ten. Vy'—he grew indignant at the prospect of the probable increase in crime which would follow upon such an unusual instance of magisterial leniency—'that ain't no pun'shment at all! If'e killed me, 'e'd 'av got orf altogether!'

Nevertheless, those ten strokes, lightly laid on the back though they were, had stamped themselves indelibly on Davies' features. And an old hand, who for a generation had been enjoying the protection (tempered with discipline) of Government, and who knew the convict nature well, prophesied ill because the lad never laughed now. There was something taking about the boy—something impressive, too, to a creature like this Michael Ferris, who was servile always, from inclination as much as from policy, in his haughty opposition to authority.

And the old convict dreaded what might be.

This man was sent with a message to the homestead by Manning a week after Davies' return to the 'team.' And while waiting for the can of tea which he was to carry to the field, the old fellow took an opportunity of saying a word to Bess. Anstey's was ruled by Bess in all things, edible and potable.

'Mrs. Sandy, a word wi' yer, mum, please, an' 'scuse the liberty as I'm taking, mem, but the men do say as wot yer—yer take an int'rest like in young Eddie Davies—'

'Oh!' cried Bess, taken off her guard by the suddenness of the remark, 'what is the matter now—is he in more trouble?'

'Not yet, missus, but I'm afraid he will be—he's so sullen like, and broodin.' He never larfs. An' w'en fellers, espeshally younkers, go like that, arter kissin' of Madame Cat-o'-nine-tail—w'y, mem, theys go to the bad, slick!'

'Oh, tell him not to brood—no, stay!' Then, fearful she had revealed a feeling for the lad's welfare that needed either instant contradiction or a further unfolding, she paused and looked anxiously at the old transport. He read her glance, and put his finger on his lips.

'I'm mum, mem—I do anything for the younker, as he gives me 'baccy w'en he has it, an' I know as the stuff must come from you!'

'Then—then tell him to keep awake to-night.'

The old man delivered the message; and he was loyal to his promise. He mentioned the circumstance to no one. But he would have been more than human if, when the 'teams' were stabled for the night in the huts by the home-paddock, he too had not resolved to keep awake.

*   *   *

Six men to a hut—the Ansteys characteristically so construed the official regulation which required that in any apartment of smaller dimensions than 12 feet by 12 feet, there should not be lodged more than twelve assigned servants. (The System would have died prematurely had the Ansteys' methods been the rule. As they were not, it was only the convicts who died in advance of their time.) The old transport was in the same hut as Davies. Even Mr. Thomas Anstey gave no second thought to an arrangement that shut up for ten hours gentry who would have rightly adorned Tyburn tree with babes in vice. It was so usual: it did not shock even him.

As midnight drew near, old Ferris woke from a snatch of sleep. Stirring in his ear curiously, was a bird's tapping which mingled with the sigh-laden breathing of the sleepers and the creaking of the pine-planks as the men turned restlessly in the bunks. He raised himself upon his elbow noiselessly and peered into the darkness. A movement in the bed-place opposite his own—Davies'—directed his gaze; and to his surprise he saw a breadth of moonlight flash into the room as a plank in the wall was apparently withdrawn. A body stopped the aperture for an instant, and then the sudden reappearance of the light, and the sound of a thud outside, told him that Davies—it could be no other than the lad—had temporarily escaped from the hut. Ferris stole quietly to the bed-place, which had just been vacated, and listened. The speakers had placed themselves against the wall so that the shadow of the building covered them, and thus Ferris heard every word.

IV.

'Well, mother,' he heard the boy say, in low tones that were utterly wanting in tenderness. 'So you've found time to come, have you? It's two weeks since I've seen you to speak to! Is it that your son has been flogged that you've discarded him?'

'Hush, you cruel boy—have I not done enough for you to show you how I love you!'

'Always the same cry—what you've done for me! Isn't it your duty to do something for me! Did I ask to come into the world?—'

'There's no time for useless talk. I came tonight, because I could not come before. Manning suspects something. I'm sure he thinks—'

'What?'

'That there is something between me and you. He watches me closely—I never come near the hut now—'

'Don't I know that? Have I not been compelled for a fortnight to live on this cursed pigs' food, while you at the house feasted on the fat of the land, and would not take the trouble to bring me the crumbs from your table!'

'Wicked, wicked boy!' There was a catch in the woman's voice as the serpent's tooth nipped her.

'No snivelling now! Have you brought any grub or tobacco with you?'

'Yes—there 'tis at your feet. God! to think I should steal like this for you, an' meet with this reward!'

'If you've come to weep over the prodigal and nothing else, you can go back again. What if you did take my trifling breach of the law upon you and get lagged—what then? Lots of mothers would ha' done the same for their sons, and never thrown it into their teeth afterwards. And if you were lagged for me, wasn't I lagged for you? Didn't I follow you as quick as I could—"Missed my Mammy, oh!" as the song says—'

'Eddie, oh, Eddie, you are breakin' my heart! An' if you've nothing to say beyond this, I'll go, without sayin' what I came to say!' Forgetting the need for silence, she burst into sobs.

'Fool!' said the ribald. 'Do ye want to rouse the huts with your —— sniffling. What did you come to say? Out with it!'

'Only this—that Mr. Manning—wishes to marry me.'

'Marry you! Not if I know it!' said the lad, after a second's surprised silence. 'He's my master now—by law, and that's the only authority he'll have over me!'

'I don't intend to marry him—because of you. I won't deceive the good man, for good man he is—'

'What a taste he has—to wish to marry you! And what a match—the good, kind-hearted Overseer, with his hide-whip, and Anstey's Bess, the lag housekeeper with the lag son.'

There was a rush of steps, and then Ferris heard another voice join in the conversation. He was at no loss to know whose it was.

'This has gone far enough, you wretch, Davies! I've heard nigh every word you two have said. Ah, Bess, why didn't you trust me—why not have told me this ungrateful scamp was your son?'

The woman sobbed now unrestrainedly. That was her only answer. But her son answered with that defiant brazenness which seemed part of his nature.

'Because she wasn't proud of me! That's why, Manning. So you want to marry her, d'ye? Well, you can have my blessing, if that'll help you!'

'Silence, sir—don't forget I'm your overseer!'

'I don't consider any man my overseer who follows convict women about at midnight, for he'll only be overseer so long as Mr. Anstey doesn't know it.'

'Silence, sir—or else I rouse the huts and order you to be chained up!'

'Do—do! But no, you daren't—you're only a coward, Manning, for all your bigness. But *I'll* rouse the huts.' And before Manning could stop him, he beat upon the walls of the hut and shouted with all his might. The uproar was increased by the cries of the now hysterical woman, and by the curses of the overseer. Within two or three minutes the forms of the startled inmates were visible on the verandah of the homestead; and there were cries of 'What's up? What's the matter?' from the assigned men's lodgings, which were, of course, locked. The impression was general that Brady's bushranging gang (then in the district, at Peter's Pass) was in attack. From the aperture whence Davies had emerged the faces of all his hutmates were now peering. Ferris had no longer a monopoly of the spectacle, which by this time was exciting.

Manning had seized the young reprobate and had forced him to the ground, and upon the struggling bodies Bess had thrown herself, fearful that the only two beings she cared for in the world would do each other mortal injury. Nor was she without cause for her fears. There was a gleam of a knife-blade in the moonlight, and Manning fell back, venting, in the instant in which he loosed his clutch on the youth, a shrill cry of pain. By the time Mr. Anstey—who, in his haste, had seized a fowling-piece— reached the spot from the house, the overseer lay unconscious, while blood poured from a stab in his chest. The transport, Davies, leaned against the wall recovering his breath, and Bess stood, dazed but erect, with a hunter's skinning knife in her right hand.

'Bess—Manning!' exclaimed the settler as he recognised first the woman and then the supine man. 'What does this mean?'

Bess passed her free hand over her forehead, and then, looking steadily into her master's face, made answer—

'I've—stabbed Mr. Manning, sir!'

And but one of the men who peered from the opening in the wall could have sworn differently, for he only had clearly perceived whose hand had struck the blow, and whose hand had withdrawn the blade from the wound.

V.

In the confusion of the event, it did not occur to Mr. Anstey to inquire what Davies was doing outside his hut at that hour. Not suspecting the relationship of the young transport to Bess, he did not doubt the truth of her avowal, although he was shocked at it. Leaving to a later and more seemly time the investigation into the circumstances, he bade Davies help a couple of free servants, who had come from their quarters, to carry the injured man to his room, where the wound was roughly bandaged till the military doctor from Oatlands could arrive. Bess, Mr. Anstey locked in her own apartment, first taking the knife from her.

The next morning the wounded man was incapable, in magisterial opinion, of giving a lucid account of the affair. His wound though not vital was a sufficiently ugly one, and weeks would have to elapse before he either could resume duty or be in a fit state to give formal evidence against the prisoner. Sitting as a magistrate, Mr. Anstey formally remanded his once-trusted housekeeper to Oatlands. She would give no explanation of the occurrence, and the family who had so befriended her, and whom she had so faithfully served, saw her taken off to the township by an escort of field police. It was a problem the Ansteys could not solve—how she, so tender and true, should have attempted to murder their overseer, who, attached as he was to them, was, as they well knew, more deeply devoted to her. Good Mrs. Anstey had done all she could to promote the match; and Bess's refusal had perplexed her mightily. And now the entanglement that bound the two was not the sweet intricacy of the lover's knot, but the gruesome ties which link the victim to his murderess.

The night after the outrage the plank in the hut-wall was withdrawn once more, and Davis, aided by Ferris, dropped through the aperture.

'It's as good a thing as ye can do, ye young whelp, ye! Ye'll get scragged in any case, and I'd rayther ye'd be scragged for bold fightin' in the bush than fer a cur's trick of puttin' the knife in on the sly!' So old Michael whispered.

The lad heard him in silence.

'An,' went on the old man, 'won't ye leave a word for the woman who bare ye?'

'Tell her the best thing she ever did for me was the loosening of this plank. She did it for my kisses—I did give her one or two—but I always intended to bolt to Brady through it. And tell her the best thing she can do is to marry Manning if he gets better and she's not hanged. Then when the —— traps are hot on my heels, I'll always have a safe corner. Tell her that—and good-bye.'

VI.

Bess was not hanged. At the Hobart Assizes she would have pleaded guilty had not the Court, very informally, and under protest from Crown-Solicitor Stephen, heard a statement from Michael Ferris, transport, and Frank Manning, free upon-arrival. But her son was—a couple of years later—on the final break up of Brady's gang.

Polite Mr. Dougherty—the Turveydrop of the scaffold—who as the law's finishing school-master put the last touches on young Davies, stepped behind the coffin (which he had just delivered to Bess) to breathe a word of consolation to Overseer Manning who accompanied her.

'I never did for a likelier lad, Mr. Manning, never! An' it's a pity, sir—I know all the story, Mr. Manning—he was so fine a lad. Had he been uglier, then all o' her heart 'ud not ha' gone into that shell. She'll never marry yer, Mr. Manning—although 'twud be a good match, sir! She ain't no woman to marry wi'out a heart; an' hers is in pieces alongside o' that stiff in the coffin. Thank'ee, sir—the gould'll do instead of his clothes!'

THE AMOUR OF CONSTABLE CRAKE

I.

THERE is a great Australian family which boasts a recently invented shield and crest. The bearings are described in 'Burke' with a rich luxuriance of heraldic jargon. Truthfully, they should be a woman, pendant, vert,[1] on a gallows sinister, sable. This is a story of the bravest deed ever done by a member of that family; which deed being what it was, is not borne from generation to generation on the perfumed breath of tradition. The younger members are taught to look with a reverence almost religious upon the inch of ribbon and the fragment of parchment which symbolise some ridiculous Imperial 'honour,' conferred for Heaven alone knows what upon one of its later chieftains, but the deed which removes their 'colonial founders' from the ruck of humanity they are never taught. The people who should teach them are ashamed of it. Which is human history. The great deeds of the world are the unhonoured ones.

Hyde Park Barracks, Sydney, in the Early Twenties. The buildings stood then much as they are to-day, where they form Chancery Square. There is, however, a slight difference in their tenants. Then, they consisted of persons who had fallen beneath the lash of the law. Now, they are the persons who wield that lash. The difference between the respective classes of tenants extend to their manners. Between the coarseness of speech and gesture of the convicts and the polished blackguardism of the present-day

---

[1] The last woman hanged in Sydney before the cessation of transportation was attired in a green dress.

followers of the Law there lies the chasm created by two generations of culture. In morals, however, there is no divergence of character.

A wall, 10 feet 6 inches high, separated at the time of our story the barrack enclosure, on the south and west, from the open, unfenced space called indiscriminately the Racecourse, the Parade-ground, and Hyde Park; on the north from the General Hospital enclosure and the pleasure-grounds of the Governor. The entrance was from the west, the gates being guarded by two lodges 12 feet square—the one on the right being appropriated to the clerks, the other to those indispensable accessories of the System, the 'freed' constables. Other offices and minor buildings formed then, as they form now, a lining to the walls, clasping as it were in their embrace the principal building. This was the main barrack. It deserves a niche of distinction in architectural history, for it was the first building, not in Australia alone, but in the British Empire, arranged specifically for the classification of prisoners according to the degrees of their criminality. Governor Macquarie, if for no other reason, deserves to be honoured in that he attempted to solve a problem which English-speaking legislatures everywhere grow daily eloquent about while leaving unsolved. If delay in the work of social reform be playing the game of the devil, what a capable partner he has in the English-speaking legislator!

The barrack was of three storeys. On each floor there were four rooms. A passage 12 feet wide ran the length of the building. Two rooms—those facing west—were 65 feet long; the other two were 35 feet long. The breadth of each room was 19 feet.

In each of the six long rooms seventy men slept. In each of the six small ones, thirty-five. As a rule, that is. But one January night, in the Early Twenties, No. 5 room, the small one on the east end of the upper floor, contained thirty-three men—and one girl. She was the founder of the great Australian family aforesaid.

II.

The grass-cutting gang had, with their coxswains, duly reported themselves about 5.30 in the afternoon. They were rather later than usual, but the wind had been blowing strongly against the boats as they bore down heavily laden with grass for the Government live stock from the Parramatta River, and such of their crews as were not privileged to lodge in the town—that is to say, some twenty-one or two out of the forty who constituted the gang—were accordingly half-an-hour 'beyond time' in reporting at 'night muster.' But the System, surprising to say, had not endeavoured to control the tides and winds—had, indeed, made no provision for such an emergency as had now risen, and did not, therefore, punish the gang by stopping their rations. All it did was to give them their food cold when the mustering overseer had ended.

'Cox'n Nicholson—crew right?'

'Yes, sir! Arnold—Russell—Green—Dixon—Hawkins—King!'

As he called his crew, the overseer ticked the names off and ordered them to pass to mess.

'Cox'n Wilmot—yours?'

'Yes, sir!' And the like routine was observed.

'Cox'n Tribe—yours?'

'Yes, sir! Hume—Evans—Grant, father—Grant, son—Dillon—Lee!'

'Right! Pass on!'

'Beg parding, sir—but I don't think as Grant, father, isn't well, sir!' The crew, shuffling off, paused to wait response to this reference to a fact they had all been made aware of that day.

'Ain't you well, Grant?' the overseer asked. The old man, who as yet was not so old, was of medium height, which appeared the less because of the stoop that spoke of his use of the sickle as a grass-cutting tool. His features were those of a weakling, the cheeks had tumbled in and the chin fell away to a point, in the fashion which, though the man were dumb, would convey an accent of servility. The fellow was a typical servant, without a mind or a tongue or a backbone of his own. When, in his free days, 'Master' paid him his wages, 'Master' owned him body and soul. And now the System owned him, and he was abjectly servile to it. When interrogated, he did not know whether he would please or offend the overseer by telling the truth, although it was patent he was ill. He was trembling; 'Grant, son,' held him up, otherwise he would have fallen.

'Are you ill, Grant? Can't you answer?'

'Grant, father,' looked at his son. That was his way always. It was 'Grant, son,' who ever answered for the old man—did some of his work for him—cared for him.

'Yes, he's very bad, Mr. Grove. I'm afraid he's had a stroke, sir.'

Grove, the Mustering Overseer, turned to the coxswain.

'Are you sure he ain't a-shammin,' Tribe?'

'No, sir,—I mean, sir, as I am sure he isn't shamming. I thought as 'twas a kin' o' stroke, myself, sir!'

'Too ill to wait for mornin' doctor?'

'Yess'r, I'm afraid, sir!'

'What do you say, Grant, son?'

'I can't make him out at all, sir—I never saw him like this afore! I'll work double to-morrow, sir, if you'll let him go to the horspital to-night.'

'Was he much short to-day?'

The daily task of each man in a cutting-gang was forty bundles, say a hundredweight of grass per day. Barney Williams, Governor's coxswain, checked the quantity nightly.

Coxswain Tribe looked around at his men. Should he tell? Grove seemed in a pretty good temper tonight, but there was never any telling how long a subordinate officer's amiability would last. Perhaps if he told the truth it would be all right—perhaps all wrong. However, he risked it.

'He didn't do nothing at all to-day, sir. The coves all helped him, besides doin' their own whack.'

'Were any of them short?'

'No, sir; Mr. Williams passed the lot.'

'All right, then. But no more codgering o' that sort is to be allowed. If the man's sick, let him report sick afore he goes. An' if he goes, he's got to do his task. An' if there's time for the others to do his job besides their own, there's time to do more for Government. We'll see if the grass-cutters can't make up sixty bundles a day, instead of forty. An' you're sure Grant, father, isn't shammin' Abram, Tribe?'

'Yes, sir—quite.'

'Fall out Grant, father, for hospital—an' pass to mess the rest. March!'

The gangers saluted and passed to their messroom. This was a long room on the southern side of the enclosure, the kitchen separating it from a similar room where the 'town gangs' messed. And 'Grant, father' stood, or rather staggered, solitary, save for the overseer, in the mustering space by the gateway. He looked dazedly after the gangers, for with them went 'Grant, son.' The younger man would have stayed had he dared, but there was never any certainty about the System's methods of interpretation. A reluctance to obey, which might have been prompted by a pure filial regard, might have been construed as insubordination. Had not a fellow been haled from that very yard to the neighbouring triangle—a statue of 'Albert the Good' now ennobles the ensanguined spot!—for marching to the dormitory with his right foot first, when the order had been given by the ex-soldier overseer to lead off with the left? So 'Grant, son'—not 'Grant, second,' that would have meant a man of the same name, but no kinsman; nor 'Grant, the younger,' for that would have signified a younger brother, whose elder was on the same muster-roll—'Grant, son,' moved to his food. But it choked him. For, almost for the first time since they had been hustled from the hulk at Plymouth to the convictship, father and son were separated. With the ship's indent had come a memorandum-order signed by a Very Great Personage indeed, requesting Governor Macquarie to, as far as possible, keep father and son together. And Mr. Secretary Campbell, who since 1810 had personally supervised every 'muster on arrival,' had ordered that the two Grants should be placed in the same gang. And Mr. Campbell was, to the official intellect, a much greater man than the Personage, for he was present, and the Personage was twenty thousand miles away. Did Mr. Campbell know the precise relation to 'Grant, father,' of the other Grant? We do not think he did; but the Personage did: of that we are convinced.

How, an impatient reader may here ask, could Mr. Campbell, who, as said above, personally mustered the convicts, upon landing, remain ignorant of the relationship if the Grants were respectively specified as father and son? Wait.

There were two parties made up for the hospital daily—one at 8 a.m., and one on night muster. If a man took seriously ill between 5.30 p.m. and 8 a.m., it was a highly irregular proceeding on his part, and one distinctly to be discountenanced. Therefore, the System would not provide for his removal between these hours. Old Grant, however, being wise, had made his illness manifest in time to be sent with the 'night lot.' And accordingly, a freed constable dragged him, not unkindly, to the Rum Hospital next door. There we shall leave him. He concerns us no more—directly.

III.

At ten o'clock, the night-constable on duty at the entrance-gate—he had two watchmen selected from the prisoners to help him—passed up into No. 5 dormitory. The door leading into the courtyard was not locked, nor were the doors of the several rooms. This was one of the eccentricities of the period for which there is no accounting. As a rule, there was a superfluity of locks and bolts, but Hyde Park Barracks, from 1819 to 1826, were never locked at night. In '26, a plot to make a sortie on the sleeping town was discovered, and then the System invested £13 10s. 9d. in padlocks of new and impregnable design—which were all picked within a week. But this is by the way.

The night-constable, Thomas Crake, transport per the *Three Bees* on that fatal trip when the mortality was so great as to shock even the indurated sensibilities of a British statesman, passed from the courtyard into No. 5. Up two flights of stairs went he, ghoul-like in the crawling pat-pat of his list-slippered feet. And at the door of No. 5 he stopped and touched the dozing watchman of the room on the shoulder. 'Grant's son—wake up Grant's son. The old man's a-slippin' 'is wind! 'E's got to go ter horspital, quick!'

The watchman rubbed his eyes and saluted. It was only a constable who stood by, but his fine reverence for authority, coupled with a profound distaste for lashes, suggested the salute. And so he made it before he moved between the hammocks to rouse 'Grant, son.'

From floor to roof ran stanchions of timber—a row against the walls, another row seven feet distant towards the middle of the room. Across the stanchions were nailed rails or battens, and from these were suspended the hammocks. Twenty inches of width space was allowed to each hammock. For some that narrow bed held a fiercer hell than even the System maintained outside, for their consciences stirred malevolently even in their dreams. For others, again, the hammock was Paradise. These latter drifted back in their visions to the scenes of innocence; to the spots untainted by travail of spirit or by sense of injustice or wrong-doing. For a brief space they forgot.

There were others still—some who were awake; who never seemed to sleep; who were perpetually crying in these night hours after their lost youth—the youth perhaps they had never known. Surely there is a heaven to give some people the youth they never knew here!

Among these last was young Grant. Amid the animals who snored off their fatigue, amid the more delicate souls which sighed remorse or laughed in their sleep, young Grant was awake. He could not sleep—prescient, perhaps, of impending trouble, slumber refused to touch his eyelids.

Before the watchman had reached his hammock he had started up. In this ward—No. 5 was good conduct dormitory—it was unusual for the watchman to patrol after silence-bell; and as he heard the muffled steps between the sleepers, he knew instinctively he was wanted. In the same instant that the watchman muttered his name, he spoke.

'Grant, son?' The full name slipped off the tongue, mechanically alert by frequent repetition.

'Me; yes, I'm awake, Butchy. Is it the—old man?'

'Yes, sonny—Grant, father, be bad. So Const'ble Crake, he ses.'

The young fellow leapt out of the hammock instantly.

'Yer'll get into it, a-sleepin' in yer ducks an' shirt, some time, my lad, if you don't take care.'

But the words passed unheeded. 'Grant, son,' was at the door.

'Oh, Mr. Crake—'

'W'y don't yer s'lute?' growled the officer, tetchy even in that hour, and though he stood on the verge of an infamy, as to a fancied slight.

The lad saluted. And then, quivering with an alarm he did not try to disguise, he pressed his inquiry.

'Mr. Crake, is father—is he worse?'

'Come 'long, and I'll tell yer!'

IV.

Down the stairs they passed, into the court-yard. As they paused at the last step Constable Crake clutched the waist of young Grant and said—

'I know all 'bout yer, m' *lady*! I've bin waitin' for this chance for a long time!'

'O God!—but, Mr. Crake, my father—is he worse, is he dyin'?'

'—— your father! Think I care anythin' 'bout the ol' lag?'

Young Grant tried to wrest the clasped arm free.

'No yer don't! Yer've to lis'en to wot I've got ter say.'

'Is—he—worse?'

'I dunno, an' don't care! 'E can die as quick as lightning for all I care. It's on'y yer as I care for, m' beauty!' He flung his free arm round the neck of the other and kissed young Grant's cheeks.

'Leave go! leave go! or I'll cry out!'

'No yer won't, m' beauty! If there's any public row 'bout this the 'Thorities'll 'ave ter take it up, an' then, m' beauty, yer'll all be in for it— th' brother yer tried ter save by comin' out in his place, an' yer father fer lyin' 'bout yer, an' yerself fer a-deceivin' of Guv' munt!'

'O God!'

''E can't 'elp yer! There ain't no God out 'ere—we all left God be'ind us in th' Channel.'

'What—d'ye—want?' Young Grant was gasping.

'Ah, oh, so an' pretty's a-comin' to reason, is she? That's right! I'll be a friend to 'er then. An' that's all I want, ter be a friend to yer. Yer understand, don't yer, m' beauty?'

The lamp by the gateway was flashing a quavering beam into the court-yard. By it Mr. Crake saw her lips quiver, but he could not hear words. They were an assent though—at least, he reasoned so.

'That's right, m' pretty. Now, yer just got ter come to me three times a week, while yer ol' man's in horspital. An' 'e ain't a-goin' ter come out in an 'urry either. I heard the report ter-night—he may live five years, but'll never do work agen—'e's goin' looney—'

'Oh!—' The cry of smitten love rang through the stillness. But there was no echo, the distantly receding footsteps of the patrol marched down by the watch-house, and answered the challenge of the sentry there by 'All's well!'

Crake stopped her mouth with his hand. 'Shout agen, yer—'ussy, and I'll blow th' gaff ter-morrer on yer all—an' th' Gov'nor can't but 'elp then but get that b'utiful brother of yourn 'rested arter all. An' yer dad won't be too looney to flog—nobody's too looney to flog. An' as for yer, wot yer refuse me, wot I ax perlite like, yer'll 'ave ter give ter everybody that axes—beaks an' sodgers an' constables. They ain't goin' ter let a purty piece o' goods like yer slip through their 'ands. An' 'tis better for yer ter 'av one friend 'n not fifty. An' I don't say as I'll marry yer, but I don't mind a-tryin' ter get yer 'signed ter me. An' then yer'll be in clover, m' missy!' He stopped to take breath, and to emit an anticipatory chuckle at the sensation which would be caused at the transformation of 'Grant, son,' into 'Tom Crake's 'signed 'ooman!' But some laughter is premature.

V.

Before his cackle ended, the girl had recovered something of that presence of mind and that readiness of resource which had enabled her, in the first instance, to deceive the hulk-keeper at Plymouth as she substituted herself for the twin-brother, who was wanted at home to keep the mother and the younger children from starving—and then, for the succeeding fifteen months, to have evaded discovery by shipmates, by constables, and by fellow-convicts. And with that restoration to self-command she revealed a sudden coyness.

'Yes, Mr. Crake! I see what you mean! An,' o' course, it 'ud be better to have only—one friend—than to be—but you'll keep th' secret, Mr. Crake?'

'O' course, m' pretty! I don't allow no other chaps to sit down in my nest!'

'Then, Mr. Crake, you can—do as you like—to-morrow night!'

'No you don't!' He swore a great oath. 'To-night or—I'll peach ter-morrer.'

'I'll swear to you, Mr. Crake—I'll swear to you I'll give myself to you to-morrow night. In the mess-room—my week for night messing begins to-morrow, an' I take the key an' give it to Mr. Grove. An' I'll not lock the—door, y' see—only pretend to.'

And Crake, whose conduct this night was the fruit of an impulse suddenly originated by the news communicated in the gossip of the guard-room of old Grant's illness, was reluctantly compelled to admit there was a wisdom in 'Young Grant's' suggestion. But he swore, with fearful oaths, that he would not only disclose her secret but would drag her to the gutters if she failed in her appointment.

She tendered him a kiss in proof of her sincerity, and was mounting the stairs again when a thought struck her, and quickly she ran back.

'Mr. Crake, Mr. Crake!' she half-whispered, half-cried. He, nearing the lodge, heard her and returned.

'Yes?—so yer thought better o' it?'

She took no heed, but went on with her question.

'Mr. Crake, I'll—give you another kiss now—two, or as many as you want—if—if—ye'll only tell me how—you found me out?'

'Found yer out, m' dear? W'y, I suspected—I'm an ol' searcher at the Factory,[2] m' beauty, an' yer ain't th' first 'ooman by 'arf-a-dozen who's come out for 'er man or 'er father or 'er brother—an' w'en I suspected yer, wot d'ye think I did?'

The girl was silent; but he laughed long, though subduedly.

'W'y, I gave yer ol' man a bit o' baccy now an' then, an' 'e peached on yer at last!' Again he laughed.

'My father—I'll never believe it!'

'Oh, but he did, m' beauty! An' now for them kisses ...'

*   *   *

When, the next morning but one, the cooks entered the mess-room, they solved a trifling difficulty which had harassed the convict watchmen at

---

[2] In 1815, male constables were employed as searchers at the Female Factory, Parramatta.

the gate. What had become of Constable Crake? He had left the lodge about midnight, and had not returned.

The cooks discovered why he had not returned. He lay on one of the mess-tables with his throat cut.

THE PEGGING-OUT OF OVERSEER FRANKE

Part 1—The Preliminaries

I.

PHILIP FRANKE was his name, and his grade was Overseer of the Outer Domain Gang. Originally a drummer-boy in the 73rd Regiment, he, by much musical beating of the tattoo and reveille, and by a fine enthusiasm in the use of the cat when a comrade was lashed to the halberds in Barrack Square, had achieved promotion in the regiment. He had won the sergeant's stripes, and with them the commendation of his superiors, and the hearty, undisguised hatred of every one—'Government labour,' soldier, or lower class 'free'—over whom at any time he exercised authority. A pleasant fellow to look at, save that he was rather undersized, he had a round chubbiness of feature which was suggestive of Primeval Innocence and Uncorrupted Virtue. No man could look more un-Systematic or more cherubic; and when Mr. Lewin, the distinguished botanist and artist, was searching for models for the group of angels he was painting for the lady of his Excellency Governor Macquarie—Mrs. Macquarie favoured Mr. Lewin with many commissions—it is not surprising to learn, firstly, that Lieutenant-Colonel O'Connell promised to send him some one from the Barracks who he thought would serve Mr. Lewin's purpose; and, secondly, that Sergeant Philip Franke was, in consequence, depicted by the artist as reposing on a remarkably neat arrangement of snowy *cumuli*.

The incident is mentioned here as demonstrating the regard in which his officers held Franke, and also as indicating the foundation for the widespread convict belief that Franke would never get any nearer heaven than those pictured clouds would carry him.

Truth to say, the qualities which were most generally manifested by Philip Franke were not such as to commend him to the loving appreciation of the 'Government labour,' or of the rank-and-file. And when on the 19th day of March, 1814, it was known that Sergeant Franke had received his Excellency's special permission to remain behind when his regiment was relieved by the 46th under Colonel Molle, there was a wild break-out of hilarity in Barrack Square, and a corresponding depression of spirits among the out-labour passports. For in the same breath that it was made known that Franke had received Governor Macquarie's permission, it was announced that he retired on pension to the Overseership of the O.D. Gang.

His Excellency the Major-General's farewell proclamation to the 73rd was read out by the Brigade-Major at morning parade. When the paragraph—

> In adverting to their Services in this Colony, although unhappily Events have occurred which must always occasion the deepest Regret, as well to the Corps as to the Major-General, it must be recollected that the Odium attending those ACTS OF DEPRAVITY ought in Justice only to extend to the Perpetrators of them,

was reached, a murmur rolled through the ranks—'Acts o' depravutty! Th' spyin o' Sargeant Franke, th' measley sot!' The files on parade had memories that at that particular moment were not to be appeased by rounded periods of glowing eulogy. His Excellency went on to express his opinion that—

> This Station has not afforded the usual Field for Military Glory, but, in as far as the industrious Exertions of those Non-commissioned Officers and Privates who could be spared from Military Duty have been concerned, this Colony is much indebted for many useful Improvements, which, but for the soldiers of the 73rd Regiment,

must have remained only in the Contemplation of those anxious for its Civilisation for a Length of Time.

He might go even beyond that magnificent tribute—he might go to the length of averring that—

The Comforts enjoyed by the Colonists in Consequence of the zealous and laborious Exertions of the Soldiers of the 73rd Regiment will long be remembered with their grateful Recollections.

But even balm of that sort could not heal the wound Macquarie had inflicted when he had given Corporal Franke an extra stripe for playing the sneak and turning barrack-room and parade-ground into subdivisions of hell.

Healing for that wound came only when it was known later the same day that Sergeant Franke was to stop behind, having obtained fifty acres of land and an overseership.

'But, O Lord, boys, what'll life be worth now for them convicts as he's over?'

This was the barrack-room sentiment. And it was not thought merely and kept in the thinker's own mind, but spoken openly without reserve as a soldier should speak. And it was applauded bravely when spoken.

For with the sergeant would pass away the chief spy of the regiment, and the lesser spies feared the rank-and-file more than they were regarded by the officers. None of the lesser spies were gifted like Phil Franke with sweet manners and a cherub's face, and consequently none could get the ear of the Colonel and the Major-General. With every disposition to emulate Franke's career as a reporter to the High Powers of barrack and guard-room discontent, two or three non-coms. and several privates had been unfortunately deprived by Nature of the qualities necessary for success. Which circumstance, if looked at in the proper light, will appear a matter for regret, inasmuch as in the barrack-room of the 73rd rebellion was always in an incipient stage, and the expenditure on a few military executions would have conduced greatly to the prosperity of the country.[1] At any time in our colonial history up to 1825 it would have been an easy thing for our Praetorian Guards to have wrested the control of the colony from the Constituted Powers, and more than one such plot had been in course of incubation within the quarters of the 73rd. That the eggs were addled was largely due to our hero, Franke.

II.

Overseer Franke was installed in office the day after the 73rd had marched down to the Cove and embarked for Calcutta. The Outer Domain Gang, as was the case with all low-class labour (as distinguished from the mechanics), were quartered on the west side of the town in the sheds that surrounded the Old Country Gaol. From their squalid living-place to the scene of their daily work was a good three-mile walk, and that distance suggested to the fertile brain of the Overseer an idea. It occurred to him the very day he assumed command, but he was too astute to play the new broom all at once, so he deferred promulgating it in the ears of the Authorities till he had been some weeks in office.

Then he enunciated it to the Superintendent of Convicts, and the Superintendent of Convicts passed it on approvingly to the Chief Engineer, and the Chief Engineer quietly appropriated it as his own, and strongly recommended it to Governor Macquarie, who was graciously pleased, in his capacity of Head of the State and Deputy-Providence, to adopt it.

Now, the idea, when we come to state it in cold-blooded print at this time of day, does not challenge admiration either by its daring audacity or sublime originality. The defect, however, is not in the idea, but in us. To

---

[1] Colonel Arthur, in transmitting a return of expenditure to the Secretary of State for the Colonies, remarked 'that every item of the expenditure would be found conducive of the prosperity of the colony.' The statement included £20 3s. 4d., executioners' expenses.

appreciate an historic fact, you must weigh and estimate it in the light of the day on which it happened. And the day when Overseer Franke generated, and the Chief Engineer appropriated, and the Governor acted upon the Idea, was the Day of Small Economies. The genius of Old Sydney in Macquarie's early years of administration was the genius of lavish expenditure, but in his later epoch, the fine old ruler worshipped at the throne of another God. Things were so skimped that even the hangmen were compelled to be economical in the matter of hemp. They wished to hang twenty Condemned one day in '21 in Lower George Street, and the Sheriff could not succeed in getting together more rope than would suffice to 'top off' nineteen. It would have detained the crowd and the Sheriff another hour from breakfast to have hanged No. 20 with the rope which had already despatched No. 1, and so, as the high functionary dare not anticipate his next quarter's advance by purchasing rope on credit, he put back No. 20 for a week.

It is from the circumstance, then, that the spirit of economy was abroad that Mr. Franke's idea derives its importance.

Instead of marching his gang from quarters to the site of their work every morning, and marching them back every night, he proposed that he should camp out with them the week through, bringing them in for muster—and divine service—from Saturday to Monday.

This was his plan. In the light of the Administration, it was Splendid, Capital! For it promised to save the Government, time, sinew, boots, money. If, in the process of economy, it also lost a soul or two, well, that consideration could not be permitted access to the Authorities' judgment for one second's audience.

Mr. F.A. Hely, Principal Superintendent of Convicts, once remarked to Father Ullathorne, Vicar-General of Roman Catholics: 'Absurd, my dear sir! You ask us to consider souls. That's your business! The Administration has to consider *cash*!'

And Mr. Hely was right. He generally was. When, for instance, he sent seventy-three assigned servants—exactly fifty more than he was entitled to—to his estate of 5120 acres, an estate for which he had paid £16 13s. 4d., there can't be the least doubt he was right. Consequently, being never in error, his opinion as to the folly of giving heed to souls when cash was concerned, must be respected.

III.

Nevertheless, that heedlessness was the weak spot in Franke's plan, as the sequel proved. It precipitated his pegging-out.

When Franke took charge of the gang there was about five years' clearing work to do on the hilly land which ran from Windmill Ridge to the South Head Road. All the area now known as Darlinghurst was then wooded, sparsely in places, but for the most part the timber was thick. The task of clearing and burning-off with such appliances as were at command of the outer gang was heavy, and the allowance of five years' time was by no means excessive for the undertaking. The Chief Engineer, however, was able to report, two years after the new Overseer had originated his idea, that the marked-out work would be completed by the gang a good twelve months under the allotted period. For this satisfactory achievement the C.E. not unnaturally took the most considerable proportion of credit, but still he did not withhold some tribute of appreciation from Franke. The Overseer, indeed, should have had all, as it was by his plan that the gang had got through so much work.

The only people dissatisfied were the gangers. The average number of men in the gang was twenty, and the official power which directly controlled them was made up by the Overseer, three soldiers, and a scourger. Notwithstanding this ample manifestation of care by the Authorities, the gang grew discontented, and had to be soothed back at sundry times into contentment and resignation by two hangings, about a dozen of imprisonments, and several score of floggings.

But even gentle remedies of that kind were not potent to keep always within bounds the turbulence of felon-spirits that feel themselves injured by three things which we shall enumerate in the order of their importance as they stood in the estimation of the genial Overseer's *protégés*.

Firstly, the gangers objected to the deprivation of their daily walk, or rather shuffle—men with single or double irons on could not walk—to and from the town barracks. They would not have minded so much had the time, ordinarily consumed by the out-gangs in passing from the barracks to the working-places and back again, been allowed them for rest. But that was not so; they had to work those two or three hours. Thus their hours of labour were literally from sunrise to sunset, though other gangs worked, say, three hours less.

Secondly, the camping-out system practically gave control of their ration and clothes allowances to Overseer Franke. And Overseer Franke, as became an intelligent officer of the System, was not slothful in the business of deriving a very substantial addition to his recognised emoluments from those same allowances.

And, thirdly, they lost the sweet solace of companionship with minds that ran in other grooves of duty, which they would have enjoyed had they been barracked nightly. 'There is no apparent motive for the prisoner's murder of the deceased!' remarked C.J. Forbes, at a later day, in the preface to his summing-up on a capital charge. 'Beg your Honour's parding!' interrupted the prisoner, with a courteous desire to set the judge—all things considered, the noblest man who ever sat on a N.S.W. Supreme Court Bench—right, 'my motive's plain 'nuff. I wanted a change! I got so wery tired of gang-work—there was no wariety in it at all!' Well, that was just the matter with Franke's gangers. The nightly chat in barracks would have been a safety-valve for their natures, and conveyed some refreshment to their minds; but in camp their speech was dammed-up, and their lips, if they did move audibly after 'lights out!' were in danger of being sealed with a leaden seal. 'Fire into the tents, sentry, if yer hear as the men's a-talkin' together. They may be concoctin' mutiny!' Thus the seven men who, on the average, were the occupants of each tent (eight by eight its floor area) were dumb perforce.

There is no tyranny like that of the petty tyrant, and there is no torture like that suffered by his victims. The very littleness of the source of authority adds another and acuter pang to the pain. Had the thousand and one miserable restrictions imposed by ex-Sergeant Franke been directly ordered by a nominal gentleman, or by an officer of commissioned rank, they would have been borne the easier. Only a man with vermin-soul could have designed and put into force some of the methods adopted by Mr. Franke for the subjugation of his men, and being what he was, he was not restrained by any regard for the common humanity which the convict shared with himself, such as even a Foveaux or a Rossell affected (if he did not feel) at times. Intoxicate a creature of his low stamp with the absolutism of power, and you would develop a wretch that even Pluto, who, so far as is known of him, has one or two gentlemanly instincts, would surely be loth to employ. Foveaux, after hanging a man in the presence of his wife and child, patted the latter on its back kindly and told it to 'Never mind! mammy'll get you a new daddy soon, p'r'aps!' Franke would not have done that—he would have shown the little one its father dangling at the rope's-end, and would have smiled as he did it.

For Franke was the most ingeniously devilish of the low-caste sons of the System that we have come across. To what degree of excellence he would have attained had the Outer Domain Gang not interrupted his official career it is impossible to say.

That thing they did: in the third year of his Overseership they shortened his official career—at least so far as the System was concerned, for there is no saying what use could be found for him other-where—by terminating his life.

Now that was unkind of the gang, it will be admitted. The amount of work done by it under Phil Franke's intelligent direction was so much larger, as we have said, than could have been expected, that the Chief Engineer had marked out for Franke in his mind's eye a wider and still more remunerative field of labour. And of these new emoluments and this deserved promotion, Franke's gangers robbed him.

IV.

There had come a new man to the gang. Occasionally, though rarely, it happened that a ganger would remain deaf to the wiles of the System, and would refuse to extend his seven years to fourteen, or his fourteen to 'life.' The men of Old Sydney held out countless inducements to Government men to extend their term of 'Gov'ment labour' indefinitely, or till it reached the foot of the gallows, but now and then it would occur that a transport resisted the temptation in the shape of scourgings and starvings to remain on the muster-rolls, and became free.

Such an event had just happened. One Saturday evening when the gang went into the town for Sunday Chapel and muster, one of the gangers dropped out an expiree, and Mr. Overseer Franke was consequently able to present no more than eighteen at the muster.

'Overseer Franke, how is it your gang is only eighteen?' demanded the Barrack-master; 'your strength's twenty.'

'Yes, sir, but your Honour has forgotten that one man got his certificate yesternight—'

'That's nineteen!'

'And one is waitin' trial, your Honour, for assaultin' me.'

'Ah, that's the score, but you're still one short, then! There, go to No. 2 yard and pick out a likely fellow.'

'Yes, sir!'

And in a second, he had passed into the inner quadrangle of the Muster-yard—some of the stone wall is still standing—where one hundred and forty newly-landed transports were huddled, pending inspection.

Up and down the ranks of sickly wretches—they had been seven months on the voyage, and short of water and lime-juice for the last month—he passed, closely scrutinising the cargo. It was a regulation that the Governor, or, if that was not convenient, the Colonial Secretary, should allot each new-comer to the work for which he was best suited. The regulation had been obeyed in the case of the *Coromandel* cargo. On the previous morning (Saturday) his Excellency had inspected the 'indent,' and had selected every man who said he was, or seemed to be, a mechanic. Then he had ordered the rest to 'gang-labour,' and thus left them to the tender mercies of the Overseer. There are more ways than one of carrying out a regulation.

'A crawling, scurvy lot!' commented Overseer Franke to the yard constable. 'I want a strong, wiry 'un, an' there don't seem to be one in the batch.'

'Try this cove wots over here,' suggested the constable, and pointed as he spoke to where a man, under the medium height, but otherwise well-proportioned, stood, the centre of a ragged group. 'This chap ain't much muscle to look at, but he's blooded—he's got sperrit, I should say, an' 'udn't prove a shiser. You try him, Mr. Franke, sir. Here, you feller, stand out!'

The 'fellow' stood. The grime of confinement did not blur altogether the fine lines of his face, and the delicate nostrils of the long nose, the sweep of the eyelashes, and the chiselling of the mouth, indicated blood and gentle nurture, while the straightforward, lucid eyes spoke equally clearly of a disposition of integrity. It was a mystery how such a man came to be included in the ring of degraded scum, possibly only to be explained by a sudden lapse into a criminal deed, or, as an alternative (of which there are many instances in convict archives), that he was bearing the brunt of some rich or great man's crime.

'Your name, feller?'

'Edgar Allison Mann,' was the reply, respectful in tone.

'Edgar *Man!*' exclaimed the Overseer, aghast at the fancied affront to his dignity. 'Man! Do you know as you're talking to a Hoverseer?'

'Mann, sir, I said—M-a-n-n! Edgar Allison are my Christian names.'

'Ah, that's it, is it! Now, jest look here, young feller, we ain't a-goin' to put up with your inserlence.'

'I meant no insolence! You misunderstood me, sir!'

'Misunderstood yer, did I! Now, wot's that but inserlence, I'd like to know? Ain't it inserlence, constable?'

'It must be, Mr. Franke, sir, if you say so; you have 'ad more experience than me, sir.'

'By my lights, my flash cove, I'll have to take your flashness out of yer. A-tellin' me that I misunderstood yer! Wot'll yer say next, I wonder!'

'That—you—are—a—blackguard—who—has—been—invested—with—a—little—brief—authority—over—your—betters!'

The yard-constable held his breath; Overseer Franke let his tongue loll out in amazement; did he hear aright, or had his senses deceived him? Did the audacious transport really mean to call him all that? The only sound to be heard in that yard for some seconds was the half-suppressed chuckle from a transport who was out on his second voyage: 'Lord, ain't the swell a-crackin' a whid in prime twig!'[2]

'Wot's that yer say?' Franke, when he had got over the shock, said. 'Wot's that?'

Word for word, pausing between each as he had done before, the transport repeated his former speech.

The whole yard looked for a burst of anger, and an immediate presentment of the offender before the Barrack-master with a request for condign punishment. A genius like Franke, however, was above doing what common constables and newly-landed transports expected from him. He knew a trick worth two of immediate punishment.

'Yer'll do, my man! I likes a feller with pluck for my gang, for it gives me som'at to do to break him in! March to the outer yard there—yer are a-going to jine No. 3 Outer, d'ye hear that?'

---

[2] 'Cracking a whid in prime twig.'—Making a speech in a stylish or masterly manner.

When Mr. Franke marched back on Monday morning to the heights beyond Windmill Ridge, there went with him Edgar Allison Mann, No. 14-736, as the twentieth man of his gang.

V.

Mann adjusted himself with philosophic fortitude to the terrible conditions under which he was placed. Reticent as to his past, he strove by whispered word and the example of a manly bearing where the whole routine was carefully designed to stamp out even the physical type of manliness, to encourage his wretched fellow-gangers to look to the future, to bear up under the infinite degradations of the present by forcing their minds to anticipate a brighter and happier time. His influence at the end of three months was extraordinary. Even the Overseer could not but notice it, and should have rejoiced at it, as in the quietude of the gang they worked better. But their superior discipline provoked Franke, for it was none of his doing—caused, instead, by a spirit which he regarded as rebellious, and by methods he considered insubordinate, and Mann's conquest over the rude hearts of his fellow-gangers was the more galling as it was a proof that he, the Overseer, had failed to break Mann's spirit in the first week of the young transport's inclusion in the gang.

He had taken offence at the way Mann saluted him, and understanding clearly that nothing was more harassing to a convict of 'superior position' than the necessity he was hourly under of 'capping' to the penal officers, he put him through a course of instruction. He had permitted the soldier-guard to supervise the labour of the gang one forenoon while he devoted himself to 'a-larnin' the gen'elman how to s'lute.'

For three mortal hours he kept Mann marching to and fro on a path six yards long in front of the tents. He sat on a stool in the opening of a tent, midway between the points at which the convict had to turn upon his heel, and every time of passing, he ordered the prisoner to salute.

'One, two, three, four—s'lute. Hand to your peak; higher, feller!' Mann would obey and proceed. Returning, it would be—

'One, two, three, four—s'lute. Left hand to left leg, right brought smartly up, an' held there till yer pass the orf'cer as yer payin' honour to—d'ye hear that, pris'ner, *a-payin' honour to!*'—he would laugh gaily here, as though to accentuate the stabbing insult; then 'One, two, three, four.' And so to the end of the walk.

After that exercise of three hours' duration, Mr. Franke turned to the transport, and said, with a heavenly smile lighting up his cherub's visage—

'And now, Mann, d'yer think yer'll know another day 'ow to salute properly?'

'I think so, sir!' responded Mann, with as sweet a smile. 'I think so! I'll not forget this lesson.' And in the self-abasement which dare not groan aloud, he resolved he would not.

He dare not groan at that or countless other insults, because groaning would have provoked the application of the lash to his back. And Mann dare not, for his soul's sake, do that. Like the poor sinner at Macquarie Harbour, who told Surgeon Barnes that once he was flogged he did not care a brass farden what became of him—he'd as soon go to hell as not—for his thoughts were hell after the lash had bitten him (Charles Buller, to whom the Australias owe so much, wept as he heard Barnes' narrative)—Mann knew he was done for once the cat stung him. He would no longer be a man—a human being; he would be an animal that cringed before such a creature as Phil Franke, or he would be a desperate, blood-craving beast. No, he *dare not* be flogged. Always he held himself up with that hope that he would always keep to the weather-side of the Overseer's mad passion.

But there was no knowing what a day would bring forth in Old Sydney times, when the monarch of the hour was a cherub of the Franke variety. Mann *was* flogged—forty stripes save one. 'That's Scriptooral, pris'ner,' grinned the Cherub—forty was Overseer's limit—''an' I'll take care the scourger don't give yer more. Peel!'

'Peel,' he, Mann, perforce did; and as he stripped for the punishment, he swore to his Maker that, before the next Saturday, the Cherub should have a chance of seeing what the earth looked like from another sphere.

The cause of the punishment was Mann's championship of another ganger.

The weekly ration of O.D. Gang consisted of four pounds of salt pork one week, and seven pounds of fresh beef the next, the flour-food being, week in and week out, ten pounds of wheat and six pounds of maize, ground by the prisoners themselves, *in their own time*, mixed with cold water.

But Overseer Franke, having been appointed, by reason of being in 'detached camp,' a storekeeper, was entitled to make issues from store to himself, as Overseer. And he would not have attained to the eminence he possessed as an official if he had not contrived to turn this arrangement to account.

As Storekeeper, he was entitled to buy, at the rate fixed by the Governor, meat, wheat, and maize, giving an order on the Deputy-Commissary-General for the payment.

As Storekeeper, he would issue to the Overseer (himself) the scheduled allowance of rations, taking his own receipt for the quantity of produce.

And as Overseer, he would issue to his men what he pleased. And he pleased to issue very little. He, as a fact, robbed them of nearly half.

One Monday an elderly transport, a coarse, languid, brutish 'First-fleeter,' working in the hot sun, fell ill. He was thrust into the shade of the gums till knock-off time, and then carried to the tent, one of the tent-party being Mann.

In the still watches of a moonlit night, the sick man became delirious for want of nourishment or from the sunstroke. Mann rose and, as noiselessly as possible, so as not to disturb the other poor fellows whom slumber mocked, asked him, 'Could he do anything for him?' But the First-fleeter, in his delirium, made no coherent answer.

Mann went to the fly-opening, and called: 'Sentry!'

The one sentinel on night duty—twelve hours at a stretch—challenged him and ordered him to stand.

'Prisoner's dying!' Mann never would permit himself to fall into the use of the corrupt form 'pris'ner,' though nearly everybody, from the Governor, Judges, and parsons, down to the children in the streets, made the word a dissyllable. 'Prisoner's dying!'

The challenge had awoke the Overseer. He came to the mouth of his tent: 'What's that?'

'Pris'ner sick in No. 1,' reported the sentry.

'Who's that talking?'

'I—Mann—No. 20.'

'Back to your bed, Mann! Wot d'yer mean, my fine swell, disturbin' the gang at this hour?'

'The man—Cummings—is dying!'

'Wot's that to yer if he is! The rule o' camp is no talkin' arter "lights out." Back—'

'You are a murdering villain if you let this poor devil die!'

'Fire, sentry! Fire!' And by virtue of the authority which reposed in the bosom of the Overseer, the sentry obeyed. He fired point-blank—Mann had thrown himself down on his side of the tent—and First-fleeter Cummings' delirium merged into and ended with one deep, low groan.

In the flapping of a swallow's wing the young convict was out in the moonlight.

'Shoot me, you murderous scoundrel! Shoot me, if you dare, and all the soldiers in the colony will not save you from the dogs. Shoot me as you've shot that prisoner after starving him—he was ill because you robbed him of his rations. You've as much right to shoot me as that other, for you've robbed me, all of us, of our rations.'

A minute of silence. Then the Cherub spoke to some purpose.

'No, no, my fine feller—we don't waste powder an' shot on gentles. That's the death they like. It's the cat as yer don't like, an' it's the cat as yer a-goin' to have. Scourger!'

At two o'clock in the morning, on the height of Woolloomooloo, with the soft sea-breezes chanting plaintively through sassafrass and eucalyptus, Mann got his thirty-nine! Thirty-nine was scriptural.

VI.

From that morning Mann changed bodily, mentally, morally. From that morning he lived only for revenge; he would not even wait to see what justice would come forth at the Sunday muster.

When the gang went out to day-labour, the camp was in charge of the soldier who had gone on duty at daybreak. This day the soldier, instead of taking his usual sleep, was obliged to continue his sentinelship, for he had to watch over the writhing body of Convict Mann and the stiff one of Convict Cummings.

What passed between Mann and the sentry can be inferred by the circumstance that the soldier threw in his fate with the gang when they made their bolt, as they did three nights later—on the Thursday.

On the Thursday night they bolted, under Mann's leadership, and seized a schooner which lay out in the main stream. Overseer Franke, of course, raised a remonstrance as to their going, but they treated it as unpolitely as they did his complaint that they were hurting him, when they pegged him out—*alive*—with tent-pegs and lines—on an ant-hill in the heavily-timbered gorge between two hills.

Alive—with food just *outside* of his reach—and a bullet-hole through his right hand, into which aperture the ants were directed by the ingenuity of one Mann, who made a sweet track of the Overseer's ration sugar from a hole in the hill to the hole in the hand.

About eight or nine years afterwards, Mr. Absalom West was clearing some ground in Bark 'Um Glen—now refined into Barcom—when he came upon a skeleton—pegged out.

Part 2—The Completion of the Deed

I.

OVERSEER FRANKE, of the Outer Domain Gang, working on the heights of Woolloomooloo, and engaged in clearing (by means of convicts' agony) the wooded ranges of hills and network of gullies, so as to make room for the perfume-breathing plants of civilisation, had been rudely interrupted in his slumbers. One of the gang, Convict Cummings, being half-starved, sun-smitten, and overworked, had become delirious in the mid-hours of the night, and another transport—Mann—had set the Regulations at defiance by imploring the sentry's aid for the sick wretch, his tent-mate. Thereupon, Mr. Overseer Franke had awoke from his beauty-sleep and had ordered the sentry to still Mann's rebellious tongue with a bullet. The sentry fired in Mann's direction, but the bullet had found its destined billet in Convict Cummings' body—and Convict Cummings had ceased from troubling. Unfortunately, the wicked Mann, having evaded the shot, did not rest. He upbraided Overseer Franke for having murdered Cummings. He became positively insulting—and was flogged.

At two o'clock in the morning, at a spot somewhere, we take it, about where Liverpool Street of Modern Sydney dips into Womerah Avenue, Darling-hurst, Convict Edgar Allison Mann received thirty-nine lashes.

And Mann was 'gently born;' and when the back of a gently-born transport had once been stained with the infamous stigma of the lash-point, only two things, if he were not to become utterly bestial, remained for him to do: to kill his tyrant, and—to die.

And Convict Mann, being at heart a really fine fellow—being, moreover, a firm believer in Shandy's doctrine that a man's name influenced his character; being, in a word, manly, lost not a minute in coming to the resolve to do both things.

'Peel!' had ordered Overseer Franke.

Mann had obeyed, making a remark as he did so:

'Flog me, and by God who looks from the heaven above, you're a dead man, Mr. Franke!' And then correcting himself, as though before he were subjected to the degrading ordeal he would assert his manhood, he repeated the words, but dropped the title. 'You're a dead man, *Franke!*'

'Scourger—thirty-nine!' laughed Franke. He might have made the penalty forty lashes—beyond forty an overseer could not go—but he read his Bible, did Franke—also the Regulations. 'Thirty-nine' was Scriptural. And it was one on the safe side of the Regulation allowance.

*   *   *

All through the next day when the only living occupants of the camp were the sentry (the one who had shot Cummings) and himself—Cummings was, of course, also there, but though he was a present horror and outrage, he was in the past tense—Convict Mann nourished himself upon the lees of his cup of shame. And the draught turned to the acid of revenge in his mouth. By the time the gang returned to work after the nooning repast, he had forgotten, however, for a brief space, his physical pangs in the pleasure of anticipation.

He had formed a scheme by which to obtain the freedom of the gang and his revenge upon Overseer Franke.

The one recreation permitted to the gangers was a rare plunge into the waters of the inlet since known as Rushcutter's Bay, which was granted to them whenever they visited the Bay for the purpose of renewing the stock of rushes which composed their beds. The sedge at that time not only covered densely the low-lying areas between the arms of the Bay, but ran out in the inlet itself, and to gain a clear plunge the convicts were obliged to advance some hundreds of yards from the proper beach-line. More than one poor devil, having got so far, thought he would go farther, and had sought to dive and swim beyond the military guards' range. If the soldiers missed, however, there were other and still more vigilant guards (the sharks), and these never, so the Authorities believed, missed their man.

On the last occasion, six weeks before, on which Overseer Franke had thought it desirable to refresh his 'labour' with a bath and with new bedding, Mann, with another ganger, going out a little further than the others, found that a derelict ship's boat had been tide-borne into the Bay, and had nosed a short way into the spiky sea-growths. Their hearts had laboured mightily at the discovery, for the fates would be cruel indeed if, with such a tool to their hands, they could not win freedom somehow. They had kept the knowledge of the boat to themselves. They had driven the craft with all their might farther into the sedge, and then had diverted the attention of their fellow-gangers from the vicinity by raising the cry of 'A shark! a shark!' and by retreating hurriedly from the spot. And all the time that had intervened, the knowledge of the boat hidden in the rushes had soothed the ache of the hearts and hands of the two men. The boat was oarless, that was one disadvantage, but they did not always think of the deficiency. They dwelt upon what they had, not upon that which they had not.

This day—a Tuesday—which Convict Mann spent in camp, brooding over his shame and his revenge, he thought less, perhaps, of the boat than he had on other days—till the afternoon. Then, the recollection flashed upon him, and, all gashed and pain-stricken as he was, he strove to act upon it. He called the sentry.

'Sentry! Can I speak to you?'

The soldier paused in his wearisome walk by the tent-mouth.

'Yes, Mann.'

'Will you do me a favour?'

'Ef it ben't agen Reg'lashuns.'

There was a moment's silence. Then—

'It's against the letter of the Regulations, but not against their spirit.'

'I don't know wot yer mean.'

'Well, the Regulation is that flogged prisoners should be turned out to work as soon as possible after the flogging, isn't it?'

'Yes.'

'Then I wish to get better soon—to get about the quicker. And a dip in the bay'll heal—the—back—quickly. The salt is good for it!'

'No-a! I'll not let yez go. Yez 'ud drounded yesself!'

'Sentry, what do they call me in the gang?'

'Gen'elman Ned.'

'Yes, Gentleman Ned! And though I'm lying here flogged'—then, for a second, the restraint to which he was subjecting himself gave way, and he shivered and sobbed—the wrung agony of a strong man's sob!—in the impotency of his wrath. 'Though I'm here under punishment, I hope—I hope—I'm still a gentleman in that I won't lie. I'll come back, sentry, if you'll allow me to go!'

'Yez u'd not get there ef I let yez go. Yez too sick.'

'By Heaven, I would, sentry. My *will* will carry me, and back, if I had no other power.'

The soldier—a pock-marked, skimpy-eyebrowed-and-haired fellow, with the irresoluteness expressed in his features of the creature who has always been subject to rule—grew dubious.

'Ef it be th' salt as yez wants, th' Overseer 'ud 'a issued some 'a yez spoken for it. I might give yez some now.'

'The Overseer would place you under arrest for stealing the salt, if you did. No; I would not ask you to do that, but the salt of the sea-bath would cure me quickly. On the word of a man who never *lied*, sentry, I'll come back.'

The sentry hesitated. If Mann did not keep his word, or became too ill to return before the Overseer and the gangers came back to camp at six o'clock, then he would be ruined. Mann read his thought.

'On my word of honour, sentry, I will be back before five o'clock. It is now about two. Weak as I am, I can do the distance in the time.'

'Strike your breast, an' swear be God that yez 'ud not ruin me.'

The crude, childish oath was taken. Mann struggled to his feet, swinging involuntarily round on his heel from weakness as he did so, and then invoking what strength he could, set out. Under some scrubby gums, offending the day with the rigidity of its contorted nakedness, lay the murdered thing. Feeble as he was and blood-exhausted, Mann spent a little of his poor force in breaking off the feathery crest of a young wattle; and threw it on the corpse. There had been no opportunity to bury Cummings before the gang went to labour in the morning, and the interment would have to be performed by the men in their own time at night.

The sound of the breaking sapling directed the sentinel's notice to Mann. He ran up. 'Yez mustn't do that, Mann; Overseer left no orders,' he said, as he pulled the branch off the dead man.

At no era in its history did the System inculcate respect for the convict dead. The convict alive was carrion; dead, was carrion still.

II.

Mann dragged himself to the waterside through the scrub and timber. It was awful work—heroic in the endurance of suffering of the acutest kind. But he was whipped onwards by the shadow of the cat. Again and again he fell; and once when he fell he burst out in a wild spasm of anger, and swore by the heaven that smiled upon him and upon the System that he would not move from the spot. He grew delirious for a few minutes and fancied that Franke was chasing him with the sentries. 'Come on! Come on, ye devils!' he shouted, but they did not come, for they were not there. And then the rustle of the breeze in the wattles and the gums, while it cooled his brain for the moment, and momentarily banished the fever of madness, played, too, its tricks with his fancy. The interlacing shadows caused by the movement of the branches seemed to him a horrid play of floggers' whips. The air was full of 'cat-tails'—they whistled, they were falling upon him, they would lacerate him yet again! In his dread he rose and turned to flee, and in the turning dashed his head against the jagged end of a limb that had been ruptured by a southerly squall. The wood ripped into his cheek, but the gashing of the flesh was his salvation. The inflamed blood was eased through the wound, and he became rational again.

He cursed his fate that he had become clearer in head, though his weakness of body had increased with the outflow of blood. And he cried against the God that would not let him die in a blessed unconsciousness of dying. But again his mood changed. He remembered his promise to the sentry and addressed Heaven once more. This time it was in prayer. He bent his head, and craved strength to keep his word. 'Let it not be said that Gentleman Ned had proved false to the trust placed in him by the miserable wretch of a soldier-guard!' A poor prayer, indeed, and if wholly sane he would have spurned the paltry vanity that prompted it. Perhaps, however, all unknowing to himself the Power whom he approached had Himself framed the pleading. The only evidence the lower-class creature, free or convict, had in those days of the existence of a Power that was true and righteous and just, was a brother-man's word. A broken vow, a violated promise—and away went the betrayed one's faith in God, truth, honour, justice, everything.

Stumbling, staggering, now leaning against a tree for rest, now pressing his lips against the exuding gum on eucalyptus boles, he went on to the rushes, crying aloud sometimes for help and sometimes hoarsely whispering to himself in pity of his own plight—moving while two voices echoed in his ears: 'The boat! The sentry!' If he could only find the boat safe! If he could only return to the sentry in time to prevent the man being punished for the breach of good discipline caused by his permitting him to leave the camp! Onward to the boat, back to the tents! Once—he gave up and moved in his return path! And then, the thought of the boat spurred him forward again.

III.

At last, he reached the Bay. Then his strength come back to him impetuously. He crashed through the reed-beds out to the circle of blue water, and plunged into the shallows. The brine stung him, pricked him— it punctured him in a thousand pores, but it renewed his vigour, and supposing there had been human eye to see, he had been cheered for the boldness with which he parted the waves as he swam towards the point in the sedgy arc where the boat had been driven in by himself and the other convict. With the boat was freedom, perhaps happiness, for the gang; and though the rush-edges cut his back and thighs, he was reckless of the smarts in the exhilaration of the conquest over himself, his weakness, Franke, the System—a victory symbolised by that swim through the cool, foam-flecked billows. He laughed in his sense of triumph as he recognised where his brother-ganger, in forcing his way out again from the dense growths, had broken off short the dagger-points of a cluster of reeds. He laughed again when the outer line of sedges closed behind his own path, as, treading water, he drove himself into the springy mass, and saw the plants which he and his mate had bent and bruised as they had pushed the boat before them. It was a note of mighty exultation that laugh— which changed in its last accents to the dry cackle of a parching mouth.

The boat was gone!

Had freedom, and wealth, and home, and woman's love, and the prattle of one's child, and all other things that make life glorious, been offered to Convict Mann the next hour as a condition of his telling, he could not have related how he reached the camp again. But at five o'clock, just when the clod's brain of the guard was dimly pondering the question as to whether it was not time for Gen'elman Ned to be showing up, he flung himself gaspingly on his rush-bed. He could have told to an interrogator nothing but the one thing—that the recollection of the sentry waiting for the fulfilment of his vow had alone kept him from there and then throwing away the life so ridiculed of fate. To march through an Inferno to reach the boat—and then to find it gone! God!

Now, the sentry could not know of this disappointment, of course. All that the stupid fellow saw was that Mann had returned, and, diverging a yard from his 'go,' he strove to make himself as pleasant as it was right for Authority to condescend to when the person to be patronised was only a transport.

'Yez a-got back then, Mann? 'Ope as yez 'ad a raal noice swim, now!'

'Oh, blast you, blast you! Go away!' the tortured wretch exclaimed, and turning his head upon the rushes, recked nothing of the anger of the insulted soldier. Which, nevertheless, was not to be despised, for was he not the representative of the military power, and the civil power, and every other power on that hill-side, pending Overseer Franke's return.

IV.

At five minutes past six that personage came back to camp, closing with his two soldiers the procession of ironed labourers. He was affable, and, as the sentry saluted, asked him how the 'gen'elman' had passed the day.

''E war inserlent to me, y'r Honour—blarsted me!' reported the soldier.

'Mann!'

In his tent, the transport heard the command, and dragged himself to his feet to obey it.

'Mann!'

Haggard with his shame and with the horrible recoil from his hope that had acted as a new blister upon his hurts, Mann went out, and saluting, faced his tyrant.

'Yer've bin inserlent, Mann?'

The transport looked towards the sentry. And the sentry then remembered that, after all, it was Gentleman Ned who had cursed him—and Gentleman Ned had kept his word—and once upon a time Gentleman Ned had doubtless enjoyed the right to swear at common people like himself; and so—

'Mister Franke, I don't wish to press th' charge!'

'Oh, very well! Then we'll let yer orf this time lightly. An' so yer'll jest dig that stiff 'un's grave for punishment! I won't flog yer agen—yet!'

Mann's first impulse was to refuse—the next to strike Franke, and he had actually stepped a pace nearer to the latter when another and wiser thought occurred to him. He would dig the grave, for by so doing he would obtain a shovel which would serve the fell purpose he had in his mind. The hand he had raised to strike Franke he carried to his forehead in salute. Franke noticed the transition and laughed.

'That's right, Mann! Yer a-gettin' broken in, I see! There's nothin' like the cat for gentles arter all—it breaks the spirit so purtily.'

At 6.30—the gang had returned from labour at six o'clock—the evening muster was held. 'Tea'—12 ounces of maize meal (reduced by the Overseer's peculation to 10) mixed with cold water—was rationed out, and then two men were told off to dig Cummings' grave.

'No. 20' (Mann).

'No. 7.' This was a feeble old fellow, one of the 'passengers' by the fatal 'second fleet'—'built in the eclipse and rigged with curses dark'—whose constitution had never regained vigour after the terrible privations of a voyage that had been one long feast for the sharks which followed the vessels' wake.

'Nos. 20 an' 7—no, we don't give no precedunse to gentles in this 'ere neighb'rood. Nos. 7 and 20'll dig th' late Mister Cummins' grave—an' make a tidy job of it—an' sink four foot!'

Mann and his co-sexton limped towards the scrub where the dead body lay. The Overseer followed them to mark out the grave. He ordered Mann to take from the heap of tools thrown down by the labourers a pick, and No. 7, a shovel. 'Ye're the younger man, No. 14-736'—when Franke was unusually genial he would address the convicts by their register numbers, and not merely by those of the gang-roll (and when Mr. Franke was genial the scourger was busy and happy)—'Ye're the younger man, an' jest yer take the pick, an' begin 'ere. Oh, it's the pick—an' the cat—as is good fer yer gentles. Oh'—the jeer changed dreadfully—'oh, help! Mutiny—'

The crashing of the pick closed the sentence. Well was it for Overseer Franke that the torture of the forenoon had drawn the strength from Mann's limbs and the oil from his sinews. The smooth handle of the tool slipped round in the transport's hands as he lifted it, and the pick struck the official's head with the side instead of the point. It was well, we say, for Franke; for the blow did not kill but only stunned him. Perhaps, though, it was ill that he survived.

The Overseer's cry had roused the guard. The few minutes that they could call their own of the whole twenty-four hours were those immediately following the muster for 'tea,' and before the nightguard was set. It had been always a thought of Franke's that at that time of the day the convict-mind was less disposed to study the whys and wherefores of a 'bolt' than at any other period, because the gangers would then be suffering from the lassitude of the day's severe labour, and the inertia which comes from stomachs filled—such filling!—after long fast. Consequently, he had never objected to a brief relaxation of military discipline. For a few minutes their muskets would be laid down by the three sentinels—their pipes would be lit—and they could feel themselves a trifle freer than the transports they guarded.

Now, by this circumstance—this illustration of his own magnanimity—was Overseer Franke undone. Had he permitted no relaxation of sentry-duty then, his cry would no sooner have reached the guards' ears than it would have elicited the speedy aid of a bullet—and it is quite unlikely that Convict Mann would have been missed a second time that day. As it was, though the three soldiers heard the sharp appeal for aid, they were some yards away from their muskets, and before they could reach the weapons, several of the convicts had rushed between them and the guard-tent. In the passing of the eye-gleam in which they saw Mann's deed, some of the wretches apprehended the consequences of the act, and, on the instant, became—men. Sottish they were one moment with the debased cravings of the creature that exists only to work, and be fed, and to sleep sleep that gives no rest; but they were men the next, under the influence of that blow for mastery. It wooed their manhood back to them.

And the guard were powerless to help the Overseer.

V.

Mann, having struck Franke to the earth, threw the pick down and strode towards the startled but pleased transports. One or two of the more adventurous of them, in that rebound towards mental independence, abandoned all caution, and cheered him. 'Well done, Gen'elman!' 'Well done, Mr. Mann!'

'I don't think I've killed him, coves,' said Mann, hardened into a vulgar familiarity of speech by the very deed which had strengthened the others' respect for him, 'he'll come to, presently. But I'll kill him then.'

A soldier—one of the two that had formed the gang-guard—at this, thought to withdraw himself quietly from the group. Instantly the action was noticed, and a ganger stopped him. 'No,' said the fellow, 'you don't get to the town. We've got a chance to bolt now, and we'd be —— fools not to use it. What d'ye say, pals?'

Then Mann knew his task was easy—even without the boat. Unless he could tell them of the boat, he had not thought to win the assent of every member of the gang to an attempt to escape. Now, he understood that they had responded to his rebellious act as tinder to the spark.

'Yes,' he exclaimed, 'hold the lobsters.'

'You won't murder me, Mann?' entreated the soldier.

'No—but we will bind you till we have made our run.'

''Ear, ear,' was gasped by some of the transports.

'We'll tie 'em up!' And, in a second, two tents were on the ground, and the lines were being cut for the pinion-cords for the military guard, who, once assured of their lives, made but slight resistance.

The whole camp of transports was now seized with semi-madness. They were a long way from being out of the wood, for, as yet, none (not even Mann himself) had the least idea of how they were to effect their escape. Inland, or over sea? None knew. All they cared to understand for the moment was that their oppressor, who was to them the only Visible Authority, lay senseless—destitute of life apparently as he was of power. In their wild burst of licence some rushed on the store-tent, others sat down to 'oval' their own or their comrades' irons. Nearly all whistled or sang. The soldiers—two tied to tree-trunks, the third supine on the grass—were amazed at the antics; Overseer Franke did not remonstrate; and was it fancy altogether that suggested there was a grin on Cummings' face?

Mann, as befitted the leadership which he had assumed without dispute, was the first to recover himself. His back was torturing him. The pain reminded him of his vow.

'Coves—mates!' he cried. 'Silence! we have business to do!'

Instantly they stopped their clamour. Two or three, however, went on 'ovalling,' and the ring of the hammer as they forced the anklet-bands out of their true shape so that the feet could be withdrawn, disturbed, with a singular sharpness, the suddenly-created silence. Disturbed also Mr. Overseer Franke. He came to himself.

The gang heard the rustle as he turned on the gum-leaves where he had fallen; they heard him moan and his cry for a drink; they heard—and for answer looked at Mann.

And Mann made due reply.

*　　*　　*

He walked up to the prostrate official and asked him did he know him—him, Mann. He put the question courteously—oh, so courteously—'May I have the pleasure of this valse?' was the style of it. And Franke nodded a 'yes,' and prayed for a drink.

'Cummings craved for a drink—and you gave him a bullet!' said Mann.

Did Franke respond to that retort? Not that Mann knew, for with that insight with which the gang, inspired by sudden liberty, had been endowed, the transports who had handled the sentries' muskets seized the weapons once more and rushed simultaneously to tender to Overseer Franke the cooling draught he had proffered Convict Cummings.

'Don't kill him, boys!' said Mann; 'only wound him!' Then—

'Stay!' he continued. And motioning for help he erected the still half-dazed Overseer against a tree, and called for more cord. They bound him to the bole, but at Mann's order left the wretch's right hand free.

Free—for a second it was. Then Mann himself took it (as limp and nerveless as Cummings' own) and stretched it outwards by a piece of line, the other end of which was fastened to another tree. The cord was tautened, and thus the hand of the Overseer was between two trees.

Mann went to the camp fire-place and, lifting a charred bit of fuel, returned with it and inscribed a circle, and, within the circle, 'a bull's-eye,' on the palm of the suspended hand.

'There!' he exclaimed, as he threw away the charcoal. 'There's a target. Fire away!'

The second shot riddled the hand, and the third smashed the wrist.

Then the leader stopped the musketry practice.

'That's enough for the present,' he said. 'We may want these bullets for living men. And this one is as good as dead!'

VI.

Thereupon Mr. Franke—whose portrait may be seen in Government House, Sydney—realised vividly his fate; and banishing all weakness—even a tyrant may be strong when pleading for his life—cried out for mercy.

'Yes!' replied Mann, 'the mercy you showed Cummings and myself and all of us!'

'Wot d'yer fight fer Cummin's fer?' moaned the Overseer. 'He peached on yer!'

'Yes?' Mann could not restrain the note of curiosity in his voice.

'Yes, 'e did. 'E tol' me 'bout yer findin' the boat. An' I gave 'im two figs of chaw-stuff fur a-tellin' me!'

Mann turned, as though he would have spit upon the dead body. But his better self was not yet dead. He thought that, after all, the System had made Cummings a traitor—and to a meanly-endowed creature such as he was, two figs of tobacco in the hand were worth a dozen boats in the sedge.

'Where is the boat?' he demanded.

Between the groans and the tears his wounds were wringing from him, Overseer Franke tried to effect a bargain.

'Will yer give me my life if I tells yer, 'an 'ow yer can get orf?'

The gang waited breathlessly for the reply of their leader. When it came, after a moment's deliberation, it was 'Yes!'

'On yer word as a gen'elman?' bartered the infamy.

A lump rose in Mann's throat. Still, he confirmed his previous answer.

'Yes!'

And the gang breathed freely. And so did Overseer Franke.

*   *   *

Then the Overseer told Mann and the others how he and Cummings and a soldier had gone to the Bay, upon Cummings' betrayal of the boat, after dark one night, and had removed the boat to another part of the inlet. And Cummings had kept that new secret, because he was to have a fig weekly till the boat was sold. For, needless to say, being a representative Government official, though the boat was properly Government's, Mr. Franke intended selling it for his own profit.

'And how will we get off?' questioned Mann.

'Ter-day's Tuesday. Ter-morrer the coaly-town (Newcastle) schooner's due, an' the night arter she comes in, skipper an' crew go 'shore. There ain't a soul on board. Thursday night—yer can go—an' I'll not report yer till Friday.'

''Ear, 'ear!' applauded the gang. But Mann remained silent.

'Yer won't break yer promise, *Mister* Mann?' pleaded the prisoner.

How the gang enjoyed the 'Mister!' But Mann's face clouded the deeper.

'What promise?' he exclaimed, at last.

'Yer promise to give me my life.'

'I made you no such promise!'

The gang shrank into stupid silence.

'Oh, yer a gen'elman—an' break yer word!' The misery of that expostulation from the Overseer!

'Blast you—yes! You cut the gentleman out of me with the cat. You die!'

And in the late-fallen dusk there mingled, curiously, the rapturous applause of the transports, and the alternate prayers and imprecations of the doomed officer.

VII.

That was on the Tuesday evening. On the Wednesday the gang had a merry day. They found the boat in the morning, and stored her with provisions from the store-tent. And in the afternoon, they pegged-out Overseer Franke. On an ant-hill, on a wooded gully-rise, they fastened him down with tent-lines. His right hand was stretched out with tightened cord again—this time to a special peg. A track of sugar was made from the orifice of the ant-bed to the hole in the hand, in case the industrious little creatures should not otherwise perceive so appetising a banquet as that shattered fragment of official humanity.

Before they pegged him out they flogged Overseer Franke.

After they pegged him out, they placed some victuals and water—just outside of his reach. It was Mann who suggested that last refinement. In fact, it was the gentleman whom the cat had robbed of his gentle-hood that devised the means for keeping the latter-day Tantalus busy while he lived. And it was not Mann's fault that he did not make Franke immortal.

* * *

The soldiers threw in their lot with the convicts. Such a thing happened as a matter of course, when there was no superior officer of the System to say nay.

And on the Thursday they seized the schooner, and, after a successful trip, reached a South Sea island.

Sydney heard of them later—when the missionary, William Ellis, complained to the British authorities that they were playing havoc with his mission-field.

But Mann was not with them then. Mann, in fact, never left Port Jackson. He committed suicide just as the vessel was stealing out of the Heads in the midnight darkness of Thursday night. His last words were: 'I've done all I can for you, coves! Good-bye!' And then he pulled the trigger.

He was privileged to receive an oration over his grave in the sea.

'Damn him! W'y didn't he drown hisself? That shot might be 'erd at South 'Ead Signal Stashun.'

Absalom West found Franke's skeleton in 1824.

AT BURFORD'S PANORAMA

I.

'LADIES and Gentlemen,' remarked the lecturer at Burford's Panorama, Leicester Square, London, one afternoon in May, 183–, 'we will now take you from the Old World to the New. We have shown you the glories of ancient and modern Italy, and have revealed to you the snowy glaciers of Mont Blanc, the monarch of mountains. Now we pass to other regions— regions where, if travellers speak truly, beauties of Nature adorn the scene that rival Italia's, where, though the art wonders which make Rome and Florence the theme of admiring myriads are absent, there are to be found subjects not unworthy of the pencil of Michael Angelo, and where, if noble peaks bedecked in eternal snows do not penetrate the horizon, there are still Alpine heights which are as grand in their cerulean aspect as Switzerland's mountains are in their garb of purity. Ladies and gentlemen, behold the magnificent harbour of Port Jackson, in New South Wales, with the beautifully situated city of Sydney on its shores— nursing, no doubt, in the youth of her existence, dreams of the coming time when she shall rival Carthage, Rome—aye, London itself.'

The lecturer paused to allow the panorama to unroll, and his turgid eloquence to sink into the minds of his hearers. They stirred in their seats with the restlessness which is hungry for a delayed delight. This was what they had paid their shillings to see. They knew all about Italy—and they were so sick of Mont Blanc—and Paris on a painted transparency, even when lit up with double-wicked oil-lamps, is no particular wonder. But Sydney! That was something new! Sydney was in Botany Bay, of course, in the land of kangaroos and convicts, where all the bad people went to when the king was too merciful to hang 'em, and was right down the other side of the world, and the people stood on their heads there, and did other sorts of curious things, getting up when we went to bed, and the savages ate them—'they roasted Captain Cook, you know, dear, at Botany Bay!' whispered a prim governess to her charge—and, in short, the ladies and gentlemen in the crowded, darkened auditorium trembled all over with pleasure as the panorama of the finest harbour in the world stood revealed. All of them—except two men, who sat almost the length of the room apart. Both of them were present because they knew something of Sydney in the real, and were curious to see what it was like in the ideal. One, of short, thick-set figure, who sat near to the transparency, gazed stolidly at it, careless of its beauties and alert only to notice its deficiencies. And the other, almost a Jew in feature, sitting near the door, did not look at the panorama at all. His eyes were fixed upon the short man; studying every inch of the profile as intently as the dim light would permit.

The lecturer began his detailed description of the picture of Sydney. As became a loyal son of Church and Crown, he pointed out, first, the Churches of St. James and St. Philip, and then the seat of Government, and became dramatically vivid when he discerned—wonder of wonders—Governor Ralph Darling riding out with his private secretary and *aide-de-camp*, Captain Dumaresq!

'See, ladies and gentlemen, look at the two brave dignitaries! They are clothed with righteous power and military costume. And, by way of contrast, see this black man dressed—I blush to have to remark it, ladies and gentlemen—in no more than a blanket and a cocked hat.' (The prim governess cast down her eyes, and bade her pupil follow her example.) 'See this black man! He is the symbol of the time that is passing away! He is King Boongaree—monarch of the Sydney tribe, and now a pensioner on the bounty of the Colonial Government. If there is, ladies and gentlemen, one thing more than another on which England has a right to feel proud, it is that of her treatment of aboriginal races. Observe how the artist has painted the Savage King—how deftly he suggests the epoch which is passing away before the new era of civilisation! See, he lifts his hat to his approaching Excellency! He does homage at once to the Representative of August Majesty and to the Age of Progress!'

The orator paused to recover breath and win applause. And the man near the curtain took advantage of the opportunity to declare in plain, audible tones that 'it wor all a cokumed job!' Then, encouraged by the surprise he caused the audience, he went on: 'There worn't no Boongaree or wot's 'is name, an' wot th' cove 'ad p'inted out as Saint James's wasn't that at all, but it wor th' old dock church on th' 'ill, an' wot 'e'd called Saint Philip's wor ak'shally Saint James's, only they'd turned it round th' wrong way! They'd got th' —— spire th' wrong end. Th' spire was th' town end—not a-facin' Park-'urds. W'y, for two balls[1] I'd paint a —— better picter myself!' Then, modestly content with the success he had achieved, the speaker sat down.

And, not to deprive the man of his honours, we must say that success was very marked. The lecturer, who had lectured before crowned heads, but who had never been lectured save by his wife, was dumb with anger. Some school-lads shouted 'Hear, hear!' an elderly gentleman hammered the floor with his stick, and the governess was so tickled that she overlooked the necessity of instructing the little girl to put her fingers in her ears at the 'naughty words.' But had there been any one to notice it, the most remarkable tribute to the effect of the extemporised oration came from the Jewish-looking fellow at the door. He chuckled, and chuckled again!

Disdaining to comment on the interruption, the lecturer proceeded. There was, however, less glibness in his utterance, and he displayed a hesitation that smacked of a doubt concerning the trustworthiness of his information.

'Follow me, please, ladies and gentlemen,' he went on, 'and notice the points and convolutions of the Harbour—'

---

[1] 'Balls.'—Convict term for 'free drinks.'

'There ain't no conwo-yo'call'ems,' interjected the critic, who, unlike most critics, evidently knew what he was talking about. 'They're all coves an' bays!'

The lecturer kept his temper to admiration, and proceeded. 'Here on this central point jutting out perceive Macquarie Fort, built, as its name imparts, by Governor Macquarie—'

'A good sort, old Locky—'

'But having been designed by a civil architect—'

'I knowed 'im—old Greenway.'

'Instead of an engineer, it is erected in such a situation and in such a style that it is rather a picturesque object than a useful defence.'

''Ear, 'ear! Yer've got it right at last!'

'The fort stands on Bennilong's Point, so called from a house having been erected on it for the residence of a chief named Bennilong—'

'Oh, Lord—who's been a-kiddin' o' yer?'

'Really'—the lecturer lost patience now—'really if the gentleman by the wall persists in interrupting in this fashion, I shall be compelled to have him removed!'

'Well, I puts it t'ye, leddies an' gents, is it fair as 'e should be cokumin' yer in a lot o' damned trash, w'en I knows better?'

'Hear, hear!' shouted the boys. 'Angcore!' cried the Jewish fellow (in a falsetto). 'No, no—certainly not!' said the gentleman with the stick, who ought to have known better. And even the governess ventured to whisper to her charge: 'Oh, I wish he would go on—if—if he would not swear so.'

The proprietor of the panorama was attracted from behind the screen by the uproar. As a wise showman, he knew it was his duty to humour his audience, and proved himself equal to the occasion by suggesting that his lecturer should be allowed to proceed, but that afterwards the gentleman from Sydney might perhaps, if he would be so kind, favour the audience with—er—a more particular description—er—of the beauties of the harbour—er—of Botany Bay. And the gentleman from Sydney generously agreeing, the professional lecturer resumed, with, it must be confessed, something less of spirit and eloquence, his oration.

'I was saying, I believe, ladies and gentlemen, when I was—when the gentleman from Sydney was good enough to—er—speak to me, that a chief named Bennilong had his residence on that point. I may be wrong, or I may be right, but such is my information. He was the first native to become attached to the settlers. He was brought to England by Governor Phillip, and returned with Governor Hunter. Although he was in a great measure civilised, yet he could not altogether forget his former pursuits. For instance, he would frequently discard his clothes, and pass several weeks at a time with his old companions in the woods—'

'They all do it—they sell their breeches for grog.'

The remonstrance of the lecturer was drowned in the roars of laughter from the indecorous. Everybody was indecorous, not excluding the school-girl.

'We will pass on. Observe this point, ladies and gentlemen! It is Dawes' Battery—mounting fifteen guns, and commanding the harbour. It is, however, inadequate to the defence of the town against any respectable force. This place acquired its name from Lieutenant Dawes, who sailed with the first expedition, and being charged by the Board of Longitude to make observations on an expected comet, erected his small observatory on the spot. May I ask the gentleman from Sydney whether that is not correct?'

'I shouldn't be surprised if it wor. But you didn't tell 'em that Black Sam wrecked th' 'Awkesbury passage-boat on that point. 'Owsomever, go ahead, old cove—yer as slow as th' Rosehill Lump, or Jim Hughes, th' angman, wen 'e turned off 'is mother-in-law.'

'How slow was that?' questioned the old gentleman, who must have been a disreputable old gentleman, thus to set at defiance the routine of a respectable entertainment. Certainly he was a humorous one.

'Well, I'll tell yer, if so be th' leddies are willin,' ven th' lect'rer 'as slung 'is patter. Go on, pal!'

Glowering daggers, the orator proceeded. But, alas! he was an orator no longer. No resonant periods flowed from his lips. If the people wished to be entertained by a vulgarian from Botany Bay, well, they might. But, as for himself, he would no longer cast his pearls before such swine. He jerked out brief, unpicturesque sentences.

'This ship in the stream is H.M.S. *Success*. Captain Sterling, who commands her, has at a late date taken her round to the western coast of New South Wales to found a new settlement.'

'New 'Olland, yer mean. The old colony ain't got a west coast!'

'An' this ship, ladies and gentlemen—this ship—or rather the hulk of one, perhaps'—here the speaker infused a palpable malice into his tones—'the gentleman from Sydney would not mind telling us what it is?' He pointed to a black object depicted in midwater off Dawes' Point. It might have been anything from a badly-drawn island to a ship's hull.

From his seat by the wall the interjector peered at the painted canvas. The audience, made more interested themselves by the accent of meaning in the lecturer's question, listened intently—none more so than the Jew-like man by the door. His heavy eyes glistened with his suppressed eagerness, and his nostrils dilated as he held his breath. He knew better than any one there how pertinent was that inquiry.

'Oh!' continued the lecturer, as the other did not answer, 'I should have thought the gentleman from Sydney would have been certain to have known that! That is the *Phoenix* hulk—used as a place of confinement for prisoners of desperate character.'

In the half-light of the hall it was not possible to distinguish any alteration in the man's features, but there was a strangeness in his voice which went far to convince most of those who heard him that with his voice had changed his features. The shock that dries the throat blanches the cheek.

'That th' *Phoenix*?—that 'taint th' *Phoenix*—th' hulk didn't lay there—she was in Cockle Bay—orf Goat Island!' But somehow the assertiveness was out of his voice, and he was quiet while the lecturer ran over the remaining features of the harbour and the town. Possibly he would not have again opened his lips, but have noiselessly departed, when the lecturer closed the exhibition by a striking quotation from Darwin's 'Visit of Hope to Sydney Cove.' But the old gentleman and the boys, aided by a falsetto from the back-seats, clamoured for the story of Jim Hughes.

He began to speak from his seat, but the audience called him to mount the form. And so, at last, he stood and gave them the story of Jim Hughes and his mother-in-law.

'Yer must know, leddies an' gents all, as Jim Hughes was Jack Ketch in Gov'ner Macquarie's time. An' Jim, though he warn't so full o' work as 'e wor later, did purty well week-in an' week-out. Six-pun' ten, in dollars, a quarter 'e got, an' all th' stiff-uns' duds—I mean, leddies, as 'e wor given th' boots an' togs o' th' free people as wor turned orf—o' course, Gov'ment pe'ple 'adn't duds to leave. Well, Jim married, but 's missus died, an' so 'e got 'is wife's mother—she wor a lag, y' see—assigned to 'im, that means, leddies, as she wor to be 'is servant. But it 'appened that th' old woman got drinkin,' an' she killed 'nother woman, an' so she wor ordered ter be scragged.' As he proceeded, something of the intoxication of public speech inspired him, and he regained part of his former aggressiveness.

'Well, w'en Monday mornin' came, Jim takes 'er out as neat as can be. There wor two men, an' he ties 'em up spick an' span, but 'e leaves 'er to the last. 'Yer slow, Jim!' ses she. 'Yes, mother, I be,' ses 'e. 'Well,' ses she, 'I allus thought as you wor a workman, not a damned codger'—a-savin' o' yer presence, leddies, she wor givin' ter naggin' 'im a good bit, wor Jim's mother-in-lor. 'But,' ses 'e, ''tisn't nateral, is it, I should be in a 'urry ter turn yer off?' 'Oh,' ses she, 'I don't know as ter that! Yer never cared much for me or my gal.' 'P'r'aps I didn't,' ses 'e, 'an' I don't say as I did. But I'm slow now as 'opin' th' Gov'nor may 'prieve yer! I axed 'im!' 'Like yer imperence, Jim Hughes,' ses she, 'interferin' with wot ain't yer bus'ness! I don't want no 'prieve at yer 'ands!' 'I don't care wot yer want,' ses 'e. 'I wants yer 'prieved for my own pu'pose. If I turns yer orf ter-day I ain't got no 'ooman to whop!' An' that's w'y, ladies an' gents, Jim Hughes turned his missus' mother orf slow.'

'Didn't she get reprieved, then?' asked the old gentleman.

'No, sir!' replied the Sydneyite. 'An' 'tis a pity too. Jim 'udn't get a second missus—it 'tain't ev'ry 'ooman as likes Skeleton Jimmy—an' as 'e wor wun o' them sort as must 'av a 'ooman to whop, to ease th' temper like, sir, he took to th' grog.'

II.

A few minutes later the audience filed down the stairway to the street. As the 'gentleman from Sydney' was passing through the doorway to the landing a hand grasped his arm, and as he turned with a startled movement at the touch, the full lips of the fellow who had been watching him bent to his ear.

'An' vat is the time o' day with you, Sam Jefferson, *alias* Dicky Arnold? He-he! the game's up, Dicky!'

The man spoken to stared dazedly at the other. The white terror of the hunted animal at bay was for a moment in his face, but vanished as he strove to carry off the incident in a braggart style.

'Wot's your game, my covey?—I ain't no Dicky Arnold or wot d'yer call th' cove as yer named—er—Sam Jefferson neither. I don't know nothink 'bout yer!'

'Vy, vot a dear innercent chap ve've got 'ere!' returned the other, sardonically. 'An' ye don't mean to turn yer back on an old Sydney pal, Dicky, d'yer? Oh, Dicky, Dicky, I'm kevite ashamed of ye!—wantin' to cut an old pal jest 'cos you're so big in yer shoes arter a-lecturin' all these city blokes an' donnas!'

The gentleman from Sydney had now regained his wits and his courage. 'No more o' this —— nonsense, or I'll call a —— trap, an' give yer up!'

'Vy, vat a bold bloke he is to be sure!' admiringly exclaimed the other. 'If he ain't a innercent, he *is* a tiptopper, an' no mistake! S'elp me, I never 'erd of a cove vot vas frightened of th' traps so, a-talkin' so bold! But if so be as ye want to give me up, vy I'm villin'!'

By this time, the couple had reached the street. The Jewish fellow's arm had gradually tightened round the Sydneyite's, and though the latter made one strong effort to escape, his capturer foiled it instantly by twisting his leg inside the other's.

'You bolt, Dicky, an' I'll raise th' hue an' cry! An' vere vill ye be then, my son? Now, don't be a fool, Dicky! I ain't goin' to be 'ard.'

A light of hope shot into the Sydney man's eyes.

'Wot d'yer mean, Izzy? 'Ull yer square it?'

'Ho, ho! Dicky, I'd 'a thought better o' ye! Ter go an' give yerself avay, like a born fool! Vy, ye do know Israel Chapman then, arter all, d'ye? Yer ol' friend, Izzy—vat copped ye at Parramatta an' sent ye to th' *Phoenix*! Vy, o' course ye knows Izzy—yer ol' friend Izzy!'

'An' wot if I does?' growled Chapman's prisoner. 'Anywun wot 'as wunst seen yer ugly mug ain't agoin' ter forget it in an 'urry, neither!'

'Vell, vell,' quoth the notorious Sydney thieftaker, 'ye ain't too compliment'ry to yer old friends, Dicky. But I'm going to do pis'ness, Dicky, pis'ness!'

'Honour bright an' above-board, Izzy?'

'Yes, s'elp me, by Father Abraham, I am!'

'Ye won't take my money an' then give me up, arter all, Izzy?'

Mr. Chapman looked genuinely distressed. 'Vy, mine friend, vat d'ye take me for? I ain't Pounce!'

At the mention of old Pounce, the Sydney forger, who did so large a trade in official forgeries of all kinds, Dicky Arnold, otherwise Sam Jefferson, started again.

'D'yer mean ter say as Pounce 'as sold me?' he gasped.

'I ain't a-goin' ter say nuthin,' mine friend—until we skevares matters, or I gives ye up at Bow-street perlice-office as a returned from transportation cove.'

'Well, Izzy, wot's it ter be?'

Mr. Israel Chapman, over from Sydney on 'Government business'—in other words, commissioned by Mr. Alexander Macleay to ascertain the destination of certain Sydney Commissariat bills on the Treasury which had mysteriously disappeared from the Colonial Secretary's office, Sydney, gave the insinuated proposal two minutes' consideration before he replied.

'Vell, y' see, there's a reward for arresting a returned from transportation man 'ere—that's five! An' then there's the Sydney reward for pickin' up a *Phoenix* bolter—s'elp me, Dicky, that lect'rer chap gave it ye pretty sharp, all unbeknowin,' though, didn't he?'

'Go on! To —— with the lect'rer! If it 'adn't been for 'im, ye wouldn't 'a cotched me!'

'P'r'aps I vudn't an' p'r'aps I vud! But I vas really in doubt till I 'erd ye tell that yarn 'bout Jim Hughes! Everybody in th' old time knew Dick Arnold's story of Jim Hughes' missus' mother.'

'Go on! go on!'

'Don't lose yer temper, mine friend! If people vat ought to keep 'emselves low vant to brag an' show off, vy, they've got to pay th' price of greatness, Dicky. Vell, then, besides, the *Phoenix* revard is ten—that's fifteen pun, Dicky.'

'I'll give it yer to let me go.'

'Stay, stay, not so fast, my son! I never does these little friendly jobs except for double the Gov'nment price.'

'That's thirty pun—I'll make it guineas!'

'Ho, ho! Vy, yer must 'ave a nice plant someveres, Dicky! An' then, y' know, there's somethink for the credit—ye must make allowance for the credit, Dicky! Vy, dis would be a brilliant capture! Vot shall ve say for the credit, Mister Arnold? Just a leetle bit of paper for twenty quid? Say yes, Dicky!'

'I s'pose I must say yes if yer insist 'pon it!' cursed the other.

'That's fifty altogether, Dicky. Now, I put it to yer, Dicky, ain't that too low for a service to a friend? Make it double, Dicky—say an 'underd—an' I'm blowed if I don't let ye go!'

'Square?'

'Skevar!'

'On yer honour?'

'On the honour of a shentleman, Dicky!'

And, though Mr. Arnold paid the notes over with a seeming reluctance, he rejoiced in his heart that his unauthorised return trip to his native land was to cost him no more.

'Tip us another tenner, Dicky, an' I'll tell ye 'ow I heard o' ye being here!'

'No!'

'Better 'ad! The chap vat gave ye avay this time may give yer avay again. An' if ye gets sent out once more—an' ye're bound to, Dicky, when ye're spent all th' mopuses on the gals—th' knowledge'll be useful!'

The contingency of another voyage across the seas not being altogether beyond the limits of possibility, Mr. Arnold, otherwise Sam Jefferson, thought the outlay of another ten pounds only a precautionary measure. So he made it.

'Vat did ye pay old Pounce for Sammy Jefferson's certificate of freedom?'

Arnold's mouth twitched in angry surprise. 'A tenner!'

'An' vat did it cost to 'ave Sammy Jefferson's marks tattooed on your buzzum?'

'Three pun' ten.'

'So this leetle trip 'ome o' yours has cost yer wi'out your ship-money, 'ow much, Dicky?'

'One 'underd an' thirteen pun' ten.'

'Now, ain't that a nice sum to pay for trustin' ol' Pounce?'

'D'ye mean ter say ——?'

'As Pounce gave ye 'vay? O' course I do! He says to me, 'Izzy, ye're going 'ome! Ven ye're in Lunnun look out for Dicky Arnold vat bolted from the hulk. I'm afraid he vent 'vay'—them vas his very verds, Dicky!—'on Sammy Jefferson's ticket. Dick ain't no marks on his buzzum, Izzy, but if ye find a Sammy Jefferson in Lunnun vith a mermaid an' a 'nanchor in a true-lover's knot on his buzzum over S. J., that chap's Dicky Arnold!' That's vot ol' Pounce said, Dicky. An' he vanted to go halves in th' revard if I cotched ye! Vasn't he mean?'

'Mean! I'd mean 'im if I'd 'im 'ere for ten minutes!'

'An' look 'ere, Dicky. Ven ye comes out again, an' I'm in Sydney—an' ye vants to make another bolt, v'y, you send for me, Dicky. I'll get ye a whole pardon with th' seal an' all reg'lar for vat Pounce charges for a ticket of freedom only! An' I allus acts skevare, Dicky—I never gives no one avay vat deals honour'ble vith me! Now, let's 'av a drink, Dicky, for the sake o' old times!'

*   *   *

Within a week, Richard Arnold, *alias* Samuel Jefferson, was arrested by a Bow-street runner as a convict illegally returned from transportation. Only Israel Chapman did not appear as the informant. Nevertheless, he fingered the reward.

About the Author

'Price Warung' was born William Astley at Liverpool, England, in 1855, the second son of Thomas Astley, a watchmaker, and his wife Mary Elizabeth nee Price. He migrated to Melbourne with the family of seven, in 1859 and was educated at St. Stephens School, Richmond and the Model School in Carlton. After employment in the book trade, Warung commenced his career as a journalist in 1875 as editor of the Richmond Guardian. For the next fifteen years he was employed on regional newspapers throughout New South Wales, Victoria and Tasmania. In 1891 Warung settled in Sydney and within two years was recognised as a leading radical journalist and short-story writer.

Warung worked for the *Bulletin* as one of its most prolific writers of short stories and political commentary. He adopted the pseudonym of Price Warung, combining his mother's maiden name and the Aboriginal name for Sydney. From 1890 to 1892 more than a quarter of its stories were written by him. Four series of his convict tales were published in the Bulletin between 1890 and 1893. His interest in the convict system was triggered by his contact with Dr Henry Graham who had served as a medical officer at penal settlements between 1839 and 1850. Over several decades Warung made a close study of the transportation literature, inspected the convict settlements and interviewed survivors of the early days of the convict system. He saw the convicts as scapegoats of English society, fuelling his own republican nationalism.

Warung later devoted himself to the Labour and Federation movements, playing an important part in the politics of the new nation. In 1893 he severed relations with the *Bulletin* after a series of disputes and became editor of the *Australian Workman* which published part of his uncompleted novel, 'The Strike of '95.' Warung resigned from the newspaper in November 1893 due to ill health and remained a freelance writer for the rest of his career. In 1896 he was organising secretary of the Bathurst People's Federal Convention which was intended to educate the man in the street and demonstrate popular support for federation. It was a huge success and 'Warung' became a zealous advocate for the cause. He also wrote *Bathurst, The Ideal Federal Capital* (1901).

Selective Bibliography of the Published Works of Price Warung

Tales of the Early Days. London and Melbourne: George Robertson, 1894.

Tales of the Old Regime: and the Bullet of the Fated Ten. Melbourne: George Robertson, 1897.

Tales of the Isle of Death (Norfolk Island). Melbourne: George Robertson, 1898.

Half-Crown Bob; and, Tales of the Riverine. Melbourne: George Robertson, 1898.

Tales of the Convict System: Selected Stories of Price Warung. St Lucia, Queensland: University of Queensland Press, 1975.

Other Titles in the Australian Classics Library Series

Jessica Anderson, *The Commandant*, ISBN 9781920898946

Barbara Baynton, *Bush Studies*, ISBN 9781920898953

Martin Boyd, *A Difficult Young Man*, ISBN 9781920898960

Rosa Cappiello, *Oh Lucky Country*, ISBN 9781920898977

C.J. Dennis, *The Moods of Ginger Mick*, ISBN 9781920898984

Ernest Favenc, *Tales of the Austral Tropics*, ISBN 9781920898991

William Lane, *The Workingman's Paradise*, ISBN 9781920899004

Henry Lawson, *Joe Wilson and His Mates*, ISBN 9781920899011

Gerald Murnane, *Inland*, ISBN 9781920899028

A.B. Paterson, *The Man from Snowy River and Other Verses*, ISBN 9781920899035

Henry Handel Richardson, *Maurice Guest*, ISBN 9781920899042

For further information and a complete list of books published by Sydney University Press please see our website at www.sydney.edu.au/sup